THE RELUCTANT LORD

DRAGON LORDS: A QURILIXEN WORLD NOVEL

MICHELLE M. PILLOW

MICHELLE M. PILLOW® - MICHELLEPILLOW.COM

The Reluctant Lord (Dragon Lords) © copyright 2013 - 2018 by
Michelle M. Pillow

Third Edition Printing July 2018

Second Edition Printing April 2015

First Edition Printing September 2013

Cover art © Copyright 2015

Published by The Raven Books LLC

ISBN 13: 978-1-62501-175-6

ABOUT THE RELUCTANT LORD

DRAGON LORDS 7

Dragon-shifter Romance
by Michelle M. Pillow

Polished, dignified and reserved in all things. That is a true nobleman.

Lady Clara of the Redding, a living statue of perfection, has been raised a true Redde noblewoman. She has been taught to never show emotion, to never raise her voice, to touch as little as possible, and to never act wildly or rashly. According to her people's custom, the new generation cannot begin until the current one is settled. She is the last of her siblings without a husband and her pregnant sisters will remain in stasis until she's married.

After Clara denies all suitable males on her

home world, her parents are left with one choice—send her to a primitive planet where several noblemen await marriage. The men hardly appear picky about their choices, a perfect arrangement for a reluctant bride.

An uninhibited woman to match his untamed soul. That would be his ideal wife.

Lord Vladan, Ealdorman Honorary of the Draig is not like his noble brothers. Adopted into their family after a mining accident killed his parents, he is every bit as titled as his new brothers, and every bit as welcome into the fold. Yet he can't help but feel the pull of his commoner past. He loves his family, and will always do as duty demands, but a part of him still yearns to shift into dragon form and run free in the wild. It is a side he indulges every chance he gets. This is how he knows his bride will be the most wild of creatures, for he wants passion, not perfection. Surely the gods are mistaken when they bind him to the most refined, reserved, frustratingly *perfect* creature in the universe.

NEW TO DRAGON LORDS?

Dragon Lords books 1-8 follow a concurrent time line. The fun of this is that the events you read in one book might be examined from a different point of view, sometimes with overlapping or expanded scenes, sometimes with events you might have wondered about in another book. You might even discover secrets as characters interact with each other. I recommend reading them in order to get the full effect. However if you bought the books out of order, no worries, each book is technically a standalone story for the hero and heroine.

Dragon Lords Books 1 - 4

The dragon-shifting princes have no problem with commitment. In one night, they will meet and choose their life mate in a simplistic ceremony involving the removing of masks and the crushing of crystals. With very few words spoken and the shortest, most bizarre courtship in history, they will bond to their women forever. And once bonded, these men don't let go...

Too bad nobody explained this to their brides.

Dragon Lords Books 5-8

The noblemen brothers aren't new to the sacred Qurilixian bridal ceremony. After several failed attempts at finding a bride, it's hard to get excited about yet another festival. No matter how honorable they try to live, it would seem fate thinks them unworthy of such happiness—that is until now.

With very few words spoken and the shortest, most bizarre courtship in history, they will bond to their women forever. And once bonded, these men don't let go...

Too bad nobody explained this to their brides.

Dragon Lords Book 9

Before four princes and four noblemen found their brides, before the death of the Var King Attor and the threat of the Tyoe miners, there was a time of peace on the planet of Qurilixen. It was not a strong peace, but it had lasted for quite some time between the cat-shifting Var kingdom and their northern neighbors the dragon-shifting Draig. It lasted because both sides had very little to do with each other.

This was the time before the great war came to rift the planet apart—dragon against cat. The only battles were skirmishes along the borderlands over territory and drunken brawls that erupted to prove which shifter side was of superior strength. It is here the dragons found their queen.

Spin-off Series

Dragon Lords is the first installment in the multiple bestselling romance series. As of this publication, there are nine Dragon Lords books.

The series continues with the *Lords of the Var*® series, Space Lords series, Dynasty Lords Series, Captured by a Dragon-Shifter series, Galaxy Alien Mail Order Brides series, and Qurilixen Lords series.

There will be more books and more series to come. They can be read alone, but the author recommends reading books in order of release.

For details please visit www.michellepillow.com

WELCOME TO QURILIXEN

QURILIXEN WORLD NOVELS

Dragon Lords Series
Barbarian Prince
Perfect Prince
Dark Prince
Warrior Prince
His Highness The Duke
The Stubborn Lord
The Reluctant Lord
The Impatient Lord
The Dragon's Queen

Lords of the Var® **Series**
The Savage King

The Playful Prince
The Bound Prince
The Rogue Prince
The Pirate Prince

Captured by a Dragon-Shifter Series
Determined Prince
Rebellious Prince
Stranded with the Cajun
Hunted by the Dragon
Mischievous Prince
Headstrong Prince

Space Lords Series
His Frost Maiden
His Fire Maiden
His Metal Maiden
His Earth Maiden
His Woodland Maiden

Dynasty Lords Series

Seduction of the Phoenix
Temptation of the Butterfly

To learn more about the Qurilixen World series of
books and to stay up to date on the latest book list
visit www.MichellePillow.com

To Jaycee Clark, it's been ten years of begging. Where is my Deadly Michelle book? Where? Oh, and I luvs you and stuff, but where is my story? It needs told. Deadly Series: Deadly Michelle. See to it. Make me badass.

And Mandy M. Roth, seriously, you're not off the hook either. King Kerrigan and Queen Michelle have been waiting just as long. Raise your right hand and repeat after me: Daughter of Darkness Four Michelle and Kerrigan finally get married. Oh, and I luvs you, too. I want magical powers.

It has been a wild 10 years since we all started together— first books published on the exact same day at the same publisher with the same editor. Who would have known we'd come this far. Thank you for always being there. Our finding each other makes me believe in fate. I'm lucky to have such wonderful friends. Hey, why are you trying to edge away from me? This speech was just getting to the good part.

NOBLAE PORTRAITE GALLERY, GREAT LORDS' PALACE

COUNTRY OF REDDING, Planet of Redde

"This is my decision, Clara. It will be done."

Lady Clara of the Redding stared at her father with a dispassion she didn't feel. The look had been trained into her since birth, the complete covering of inner emotions, the stoic nature and unmoving enthusiasm. *Not* that she was feeling anything close to enthusiasm. In fact, it was quite the opposite. She had once seen a maid screaming and kicking her limbs about in a very public display, highly inappropriate and exactly what Clara felt on the inside. She never did discover exactly what had gotten the maid so upset. Perhaps something inside the woman had simply broken. Whatever it was, the maid had never been heard from again after the enforcement officers took her away.

Clara took a deep breath and then another before locking eyes with her reflection on the mirrored wall. The purple gaze stared back at her from beneath the tall white wig that covered her blonde locks. The tight bodice of her gown was impeccably sewn, leading into the wide hoop of her skirts. She stayed perched on the very end of her seat, balancing with ease. A lady's back never touched a chair, nor her hands the arms of the furniture. In fact, her hands rarely touched anything. Clara was an ornament, a lady. She was allowed to have a mind, so long as she looked beautiful and refined and did not speak her thoughts out of turn. There were designated times and places for intellect, and there were times and places for silence. Decorum had many rules and she followed them all, naturally, regally, unwaveringly. She had no choice, for she was born a lady, raised a lady, and would forever be a lady.

The gilded frames of the mirrors shone with tiny hints of light along their carved lengths. The beauty of the detail was lost on her even as it caught her brief attention. Family portraits lined the walls, seeming to disappear down an endless walkway. With each generation, the hall became longer, until every member of the family was cataloged in such a way as to mark their importance as a whole.

Finally, after the proper amount of required contemplation, she looked at her father. His powdered wig and long jacket matched hers in design, down to the delicate floral embroidery along the hemlines. He traced a finger over the back edge of a chair. Men on her planet did not have the burden of sensitive hands.

Softly, she answered in an even tone, "I must protest, Father. I have looked at the planetary information and the location is unacceptable. Surely such a choice does not do honor to my name."

"Perhaps you should have thought about that before you rejected the twenty suitors presented to you at the last ball. You act as if nobility grows in the garden spot to be chosen and plucked at whim. Your sisters were able to find men from noble households. It is time for you to do the same. We have these laws for a reason."

Marriage laws. What a joke. No one could even tell her the reason for them, only that they were as they always had been. Her history lessons spoke of a population issue due to fratricide, and she deduced that maybe generations were started around at the same time and only after everyone was wed to avoid issues of inheritance. Unmarried children were particularly troublesome to Redding's complicated inheritance laws, especially if they were multigenerational. Her people preferred matters to be well organized. When she'd asked her tutor, he'd seemed disinterested in discussing an answer.

The only way she would get out of marriage was if every unmarried male creature of recognized noble birth were to suddenly die so she could participate in a spirit marriage and become an instant widow. In the old days, that wasn't so hard. But now, with interplanetary travel and medical advancements that extended her people's lives into the hundreds of years? A plague would have to sweep through all the known universes before she could get out of marriage duty. Clara thought of her nineteen sisters. Out of all of them, only three had what she would call a good marriage—not great, but decent enough.

"Why can't we change the laws? I see no reason why I must marry just so my sisters may be let out of stasis to have children. Wake them up and let them have children now. I will revoke my right to marriage and procreation," Clara said, not swaying on the end of her cushioned seat. The words themselves were bold. Having anything less than ten children was frowned upon in a noble family, but no children? Unless she had medical clearance, in which case they would pity her unbearably, no children at all was a dishonor.

Instantly, she wished she could take the words

back, but she remained calm and didn't let her penitence show. If anyone walked by they would surely think her made of marble and carved into still perfection. Her face was made pale by the sheen of cosmetics with bright lips and cheeks that did not occur naturally on her world. Her lashes and brows were coated with purple to match her eyes.

"There can be no children until the current generation is settled. You know the laws," her father snapped. His words became a low, even tone of warning. "Twelve of your sisters sleep, waiting on you to marry, and the others will soon join them. You are the daughter to the Great Lord of the Redding. There is but one higher rank on this planet. How would it look if our family was to disregard the marriage laws, the custom of our very people, to accommodate the whim of one young lady who thinks herself above marriage? You keep an entire generation of my line from being born. I would have my grand-children!"

Clara felt a small tremor as he raised his voice. Rarely did her father speak to her thus. She saw his hands tremble with rage and knew she had pushed him too far. "Forgive me, Great Lord, for showing my fear of off-world travel. I do not think myself above our people. I plead with you to find another way. Do not make me go to Qurilixen. Even the name is hard on the tongue."

"It has been decreed and you have the emperor's blessing. In less than a month's time, they will have their yearly marriage ceremony. Four princes and several Draig nobles will be in attendance. I am assured you may have your pick of any one of them. You will arrive when the other potential brides do, but you will be in your own transport. I see no reason for you to travel with the commoners. The Draig king knows of your arrival and arrangements have been made that you only be presented before those of noble birth before the other women have a chance at them. Choose whomever you like. I have it on authority the men will not protest once a lady makes her decision."

"But they do not decide beforehand who they will marry? They simply choose that night out of a group of women? It is barbaric."

"It is how they do things. What does it matter? You decided against your suitors with one meeting. The Draig men decide for their suitors in one meeting. And, if they are as barbaric as you have deduced in these few moments of hearing about them, then you should have no problem maintaining control over your spouse. You are a lady. How hard is it to assert authority over a barbarian? So long as he is a nobleman, our laws are satisfied.

I am sure you will have your pick, Clara. You have always had a discerning eye and I doubt a primitive man will be able to resist your decree once you decide you will have him. Go. Choose your husband. Your marriage will let your sisters out of stasis. I will have my grandchildren. Live with the barbarian lord for a year and then come home if you wish to have your first child here. Then you will go back, get pregnant again and return. We will raise the children nobly and measures will be taken to ensure they are not barbaric in nature, so rest easy on that account. Once you have given five live births, if you still do not like your primitive husband, manage the problem. But you will marry. Let your sisters have their babies. Let the next generation begin."

"Five?" Clara took a slow deep breath. The amount still felt like a high number when faced with her current situation, but it was hardly a respectable amount. Perhaps her father believed if he got her to agree to that much, she would then be persuaded later to contribute a more honorable number to the family line.

"Your sisters will gladly have more children to cover where you do not."

Even the way he said it made her ashamed of herself. The guilt she tried hard to suppress welled up inside her.

"They will be happy they are finally able to bring about the new line." The great lord paused before quietly adding, "And we are unsure how the blended bloodline will turn out. Best not to have too many."

She again thought of that maid, screaming and flailing her limbs. Clara nodded once at her father's expectant look and merely sat.

Nineteen sisters. Eleven brothers. A noble father. A noble mother. They all waited on Clara, the last of the Redding line to find a spouse. She had known as she sent the last suitors away that she took a risk. But how could she marry Lord Camern? He was in love with himself. And Camern's brother, Lord Dane? Dane was not-so-secretly in love with Clara's brother.

"And if they do not accept me?" Even as she asked it, Clara didn't consider it a real possibility. She knew her worth. She was told she was beautiful. She had money. Her family had power. She had refinement. Any man would be lucky to have her. Besides, experience had taught her that noblemen were not so picky when it came to doing their duty of marriage.

Was it wrong that sometimes, in the night when she was alone, she imagined a different kind of marriage? One where talk was not focused around having the next generation?

"Then do not come home." The threat was clear. If she didn't do as decreed, she would be exiled. Penniless. Powerless. To come back unmarried would mean death.

One year with a primitive man suddenly didn't sound so hard. Her father said five children, but she could find a way to stop after three, when the newness of her marriage announcement was forgotten for other gossip. One year off-world. Two well-timed trips back. Three children. Perhaps the barbaric husband wouldn't be too bad. Perhaps she would find someone refined and willing to learn whatever etiquette he did not already possess. And then there was that tiny hope she dared not dwell on—perhaps she would like this new world, perhaps there she could find something she did not have in her current life.

Clara closed her eyes and slowly nodded. "I will do what you wish, Father. Always as you wish."

"I will inform the family," he said, standing quickly. "They will be much relieved to hear of your sensibility. I am sure your mother will wish to shop as she did with your sisters. Stay where you are. I will send her to you."

"Yes, Father," Clara answered in the same even tone. "I will do what you wish."

Clara didn't move, merely stared at her reflection and the scene surrounding her. She looked like one of the paintings. The room was impeccable, from the large oval frames spaced evenly apart to the golden rail used to hold people back from the wall. Three times a year, people would come to the house to walk through the portrait hall and see the glory of her family.

A family that cannot continue if I do not do this.

Clara felt the sorrow and fear and pushed it deep into the pit of her stomach.

"Joyous daughter! The great lord has told me of your reasoning." Jaene, the Great Lady of the Redding, looked like an aged version of her unmarried daughter, though the thick cosmetics on her face smoothed the wrinkles and hid the tired lines Clara knew to be there. Though the gemstones on her mother's gown probably weighed nearly thirty pounds, the woman moved under the burden with ease and grace. "I will mourn your going."

Clara didn't think her mother looked too mournful. In fact, her eyes looked relieved, as if finally her duties were finished as she sent the last daughter off. The fact that she didn't have to plan a wedding celebration on planet was a bonus.

"And I will mourn going," Clara said, standing. Her own gown was heavy, but not nearly as heavy as the great lady's. When they faced each other, the full skirts kept them from getting too close.

"No, no, you must not. You must smile and

accept your new husband's home world." Her mother lifted her wrist to hover before Clara's eyes in a loving gesture. She saw the thin blue veins, so familiar to her. They were unchanged since Clara's youth when she and her siblings had been filtered through the hall for the daily greeting of their parents. Without touching her daughter's perfectly painted face, Jaene let the gesture drop. Clara repeated the movement with her own wrist, holding it before her mother. Decorum dictated they did not touch. The rush of feelings caused by skin contact would become overwhelming to their senses. The smell of their perfume lingered in the air. Then, dropping her hand gracefully to her side, she stood calmly and waited.

"We must prepare you," Jaene continued. "Come. The seamstresses have been working on the Qurilixen native garb for your trousseau, and your father has requested the cobbler reline your trunk so you may hide jewels and space credits. I will not have my daughter without means."

The words said more than her mother ever would admit to. Clearly, Clara's planned nuptials had been in the works for some time if clothes and a new truck lining had been ordered. And, if they worried about her means, that meant they did not think her new home was to be very refined.

A small shiver of fear worked up Clara's back

and her feet would have stumbled if not for the balancing weight of the dress. She followed her mother through the wide doors, not touching the frame or the walls. Only her feet and the brush of her hemline touched the floor. Her steps were short but fast, the tall boots whispering on the hard marble.

Her mother came to a glass and gold enclosure, stepped in and rode the cage up to the fourth floor before sending it down for her daughter. Clara stepped inside, turning to watch the hall disappear under her feet. The enclosed space felt tighter than usual and she began to pant for air. Was it her imagination, or was the cage not moving? Her head began to spin. She blinked, trying to focus her suddenly blurry vision. Her heart pounded, harder and louder than she ever remembered it beating before, not counting her exercise time. She lifted her hands, almost touching the glass before she caught herself and drew them to her waist. The cage stopped moving to let her out, but she couldn't force herself to walk.

"Clara? Clara!" her mother insisted under her breath behind her.

Clara jolted in surprise and turned to see the woman frowning in disapproval. "Monitor yourself and meet me in the fitting room. I will prepare the seamstresses."

"Yes, Great Lady," Clara mouthed more than whispered.

Her mother hurried away to give her daughter privacy to recover.

DRAIG ROYAL PALACE, Planet of Qurilixen

In light of his three older brothers' foul moods, Lord Vladan, Ealdorman Honorary of the Draig, tried to contain his excitement from them. It was difficult. Tonight he would finally join the grooms in search of a bride in what was to be his first, and gods willing, *only* marriage ceremony.

It was possible that, in mere hours, as he stood in the receiving line watching the alien women walk passed him, he would find the one he was destined by the gods to marry. He'd imagined the ceremony many times. He would see her, and with that first glance the crystal hanging from his neck would begin to glow, showing him his destiny. Many husbands claimed to instinctively know who their brides were seconds before the gods' will was confirmed by the sacred stone. Would he? Would he feel her as if she were part of himself? Anticipation and excitement built within him. He did his duty. He made his offerings. Surely the gods would bless him.

Vlad couldn't blame his brothers for their lack of enthusiasm. Fate had been harsh to the other three. This wasn't their first Breeding Festival in search of a wife.

For the eldest of them, Bron, this night marked his seventh attempt at finding a bride. Vlad couldn't imagine having to wait, and hope, for seven long years. It was no wonder the high duke was in a vile mood. The second oldest, Alek, faced his fifth attempt at finding a mate, and Mirek his fourth. Vlad tried not to let their cynicism get the best of him, even as he was forced to hide his excitement from them. They had every right to be cynical. He just didn't wish to give up before he had even tried.

Vlad, like every other Draig man, wanted to be blessed with a wife. Women were scarce on their planet due to the blue radiation of the three suns. Over the generations, it had altered the men's genetics to produce only strong male warriors. Maybe once in a thousand births was a Qurilixian female born. In the old days, the Draig men had used portals to snatch brides from their homelands and bring them back to Qurilixen. Those portals were now lost. There were rumors their people originated on a planet called Earth, a planet populated with more women than men, but there was no remaining proof, only stories.

Still, they were men and men must find their brides somehow. It was their duty to marry and have children, to carry on the family name and the Draig culture. But, more selfishly, they yearned for their other half—a woman to hold and protect, to love and cherish, to experience and enjoy. Without love, life was nothing but endless tasks and battles.

The fact the Draig had next to no women of their own was why the services of bride procurement corporations like Galaxy Brides were so invaluable. In return for the corporation finding and transporting willing women to the planet in hopes of marriage, the Qurilixian would mine valuable metal that was only found in their caves. The metal was a great power source for long voyaging starships, all but useless to the Qurilixian, who preferred living as simply as possible. It was Vlad's job to oversee the mines, make sure the workers were well cared for, that production stayed on schedule and the needs of all were met. In this task, he worked closely with his brother Lord Mirek, the mining ambassador.

Turning his attention to his uncle, King Llyr of the Draig, Vlad tried to pay heed to the man's words. He had traveled south with his brothers from their home in the mountains to attend the ceremony. It was the one night a year that darkness fell on the normally bright planet, and the only time men were allowed to marry. Absently, he touched the sacred crystal hanging around his neck. This time tomorrow it could be broken in tiny pieces, sealing his union. On the day he was born, his father had journeyed to Crystal Lake, dove beneath the waves and pulled the stone from the earth. Vlad, like all Draig, had worn the crystal ever since. But it wasn't just a custom. It was how they received the will of the gods.

"I see not all of you have come with sour hopes," the king said, grinning at Vlad's vacant expression.

Vlad chuckled, not bothering to deny his daydreaming. There was no shame in wishing for a life mate. What good was living if a man didn't have a family?

"It is good to see you boys," the king continued. They could be three hundred years old and the king would still call them boys. They were younger than the king's sons by a few years, but not so much that it mattered. "How fares the kingdom in the north?"

"All is well," Bron answered.

"And the mines?" King Llyr asked.

"Standing," Vlad said.

"Negotiations?" The king turned his attention to Mirek.

"Slow, but in such there is normalcy," Mirek

said. "I have brought Prince Olek a proposal document from the Lithor Republic. I have done what I can, but they insist on having a member of the royal family for the final negotiations."

"Good. Good. The queen will be pleased to hear of the progress with the Lithorians." The king nodded. Then, to the last brother he asked, "And the herd?"

"I have a mare about to drop," Alek answered. As Top Breeder on the planet, Alek's whole life focused around the ceffyl mares and steeds. The animals carried supplies for the soldiers, helped the farmers, provided planetary travel and in very extreme times were used for meat. Unfortunately, they had a gestation period of three years and only about half of the pregnancies made it to term. "I plan to leave as soon as possible to attend the birth."

The king nodded, knowing the importance of such a task. "Let us hope your bride is willing for a quick journey, but if she is not, let her stay behind with your brothers and they shall bring her to you at a more leisurely pace."

Alek nodded but didn't answer. Vlad knew the man didn't think marriage likely.

What had they told him just moments before entering the king's hall?

If you do not find a bride, let no emotion show on your

face. You will want to scream to the gods your disappoint-ment. However, others will be looking to us to know how to act.

If you do not find a bride, we will gather at the cliff campsite so that we can depart first thing after the ceremonies are completed. Trust us. You will not feel much like joining the celebration below. Drink with your brothers instead. It is not so bad sleeping under the night sky.

If you do not find a bride...

If you do not find a bride...

If...

Vlad could well translate their meaning. They had been saying things like that the whole trip down the mountains, preparing him for the disappointment they believed was to come. He knew they meant well, but he did not want his first time at the festival to be dampened by their moods. Where they felt resignation, he felt hope. He wanted to find a wife, wanted to look upon the faces of the women who'd come to them.

The brides knew they came for marriage and were willing to accept who fate chose for them. He had pictured the type of woman he'd be blessed with, fantasized about her, not only in the bedroom but in everyday activities—hiking and camping in the forest, hunting and training, running through the mountains at full speed until sweat and dirt marred their bodies. She would be tough and wild, sparring with him one minute and aggressively making love to him the next. She would take on mountains and hard rapids. She would escape the drudgery of nobility with him and they would go to the forest every chance they got. He could imagine no other kind of bride, for those were the things he loved. Those were the things he'd prayed diligently for.

Vlad smiled. *An untamed soul for my untamed soul.*

"Now that business is attended to, sit, eat." The king gestured to a nearby table. They were in the main hall where the palace inhabitants normally gathered to dine. The red stone floor was swept clean. The room had steeply arched ceilings with the center dome for light. Banners of the family crest lined the walls, one for each color of the soon-to-be family lines of his cousins—green for Prince Olek, red for Prince Zoran, black for Prince Yusef and blue-gray for Prince Ualan. Each banner had the embroidered silver symbol of the dragon.

Lines of tables reached across the floor but were currently empty. The king waved to servants, directing them to serve the visitors. As if anticipating the order, two men came into the room carrying pitchers and goblets and set them out on the table.

When the servants retreated, the king said, "Your cousins will be in to greet you shortly.

Perhaps your calm can settle their spirits. They bounce around here like children about to get a new sword." Though the man grumbled, his own steps had a decisive air of excitement to them as he left the brothers alone.

Outside the mountain fortress palace, the festival grounds were being constructed in a wide valley filled with pyramid-shaped tents and decorated by waving banners. Servants busily worked to make sure everything was in order before the Galaxy Brides' shipment arrived. Vlad wondered if the festival was always so big. In previous years, he had been too busy to join the festival as an observer. He'd been needed to attend the mines, or to entertain intergalactic diplomats, or once to even direct the cleanup after a fire took most of their castle's kitchen. To hear his brothers describe it, the ceremony was hardly worth mentioning.

Perhaps the scale of the ceremony this year was due to the fact that their cousins, the royal Princes of Draig, were scheduled to attend—all four of them in their first ceremony. Vlad especially looked forward to seeing Prince Yusef. They shared much of the same mentalities—uncomplicated living, a love for the outdoors, an easygoing nature that did not thrive on the usual pomp and circumstance of nobility. They often tracked *baudrons* together in the north hunting grounds. Yusef would understand

and perhaps share in his excitement, whereas his brothers did not.

Vlad wanted to tell them not to bother waiting for him, that he and his new bride would spend a few days at the palace, but as he looked at their quiet faces, he felt the first true pang of worry deep in his gut. What if he didn't find someone? What if in seven years he was sitting right in this spot, trying not to think of the pyramid tents being erected and warning others not to expect too much from this ceremony?

His heart beat harder and his stomach knotted into a tight ball. Excitement turned to worry, which tried to turn into fear. But Vlad was a warrior first, as were all the Draig, and warriors did not give in to fear and doubt. Tonight he would find a wife. He had to. His heart would not accept failure.

2

"I UNDERSTAND what I ask of you is highly unusual," the king said to his four sons and four nephews. They stood, already dressed for the night's ceremony though dusk still had hold of the countryside. A long white tent had been constructed near the palace, away from the bridal tents dotting the valley below. The arrangement the king proposed was indeed highly unusual.

The Galaxy Bride's ship hovered in the sky, making the necessary maneuvers to land the large space craft on its designated field. Inside, the craft was full of women—women just waiting to join with a husband. It took all of Vlad's willpower not to look up at the sky like a starving man seeing a loaf of blue bread.

The king's continued words drew Vlad's attention back to the white tent. "However, Lady Clara of the Redding comes from a family of strict customs." His uncle wore an odd expression, as if he would say more but thought better of it. "Her traditions dictate she only marries into nobility or royalty, and she is not to intermingle with the other unmarried women. Should she not find her match, she will be escorted back to her ship and will forgo attending tonight's ceremony. Her people have agreed that, should she marry tonight, from that point on she will recognize our customs as her own, as she will then be given over to our care."

"I have never heard of such an agreement," Prince Ualan said. "Why would she not wish to meet all the bachelors? How is she to know the will of the gods if she does not?"

"I would hate to think some man goes without a wife because this Clara would not marry beneath her station," Prince Yusef added.

"The reason we have these ceremonies is that all are equal. Decisions are made by fate, not power or money or a man's position," Bron agreed. "I find this odd."

"Then fate will decide if she is meant to be with any of you or none," the king interrupted the discussion starting between the grooms. "The gods have entrusted we elders to be their voices and, in this matter, we have decided to respect the culture of Lady Clara's people. She is inside this tent. It is my command that you be presented to her." He gave a pointed look to the three men who had failed to find a wife at previous ceremonies.

Alek lifted his chin stubbornly. Bron frowned. Mirek kept his eyes on the tent.

"I see no reason not to try," the king insisted.

All of the grooms shared looks and slowly began to put the traditional leather mask over their features to hide their faces from forehead to upper lip. As was customary for the grooms, they all wore a fur loincloth, a gold band around their biceps, the mask and their sacred crystals around their necks. The outfits were to make nobles indistinguishable from peasants—though in this instant it didn't seem to matter. Lady Clara knew she was only being presented to nobles. However, choosing a marriage partner was not about such things as power and money and position. It was about compatibility, fate, destiny, the will of the gods.

Vlad had his doubts about meeting Lady Clara like this, but not to the extent the others were expressing. The odds were slim that the gods would choose her to be his wife out of all of the other women coming to his planet. He looked up at the bridal ship. It was closer now, the bottom of it hidden by the tops of the giant forest trees surrounding the valley.

Mirek nudged his shoulder, drawing his attention to the fact he was supposed to be following his cousins into the tent. He gave a rueful grin and moved toward the entrance. Soon. Fate would bless him with a bride very soon. He could feel it.

"I CANNOT WEAR THAT GOWN." Clara looked at the practically nonexistent garment and then dismissed it with a deliberate turn of her body. The traditional Qurilixian dress was constructed of a soft material with a natural sheen. Problem was there wasn't enough of the slinky stuff to cover her entire body. In fact, it was only a couple of small rectangles of material with a few straps that went in so many directions she wasn't sure how to even put the thing on. And, if by some miracle she made it into the gown, the tight fit wouldn't leave much of her body to the imagination. Besides, the width of the Redding skirt would keep them at a respectable distance. She didn't want to risk accidental skin contact.

Clara kept her hands at her sides and took her eyes from the offensive dress. It might be this primitive planet's custom, but there was no way in all of the known galaxies that she would be showing anyone, let alone strangers, such an inappropriate amount of flesh. "I am sure my noble mother knew nothing of its construction. I will simply manage with what I now wear."

"We were ordered to prepare you as per the custom of the planet," Eula protested. The traveling companion moved to lift the garment toward her mistress. "Your mother wishes for you to have every advantage of making this work."

The words were like a slap in the face, though Clara did not acknowledge the unintentional insult. It wasn't Eula's fault that Clara's unmarried status and situation was publicly known. The commoners did like their noble gossip.

Confronted with the offensive garment yet again, Clara glanced down at it. "I am not like the common brides being presented later this evening. I will not compromise myself or etiquette by putting that on." Her gaze traveled to the two small slippers that matched the bridal gown. "I will, however, compromise by wearing the shoes. You may unlace my boots and put them on me."

She didn't mean to sound so demanding, but her emotions were beginning to churn and she was having a hard time keeping them suppressed. Unhampered emotions led to chaotic thoughts, and she would not put the burden of her feelings on Eula. The woman might not have the same level of sensitivity that ran in Clara's family line, but the servant would be able to detect Clara's emotions if the lady allowed herself to feel them.

Clara sat on a low bench, balancing easily as Eula began the slow process of unlacing a boot. The footwear went all the way up her thigh, hugging tight to her legs. With the weight of the jeweled gowns, the boots were useful in keeping a lady on her feet. They braced the muscles, supporting them during a long day of standing still.

The servant was careful not to press her palms forward, using only the tips of her fingers to work. To dull their sensitivities, many commoners would rub sand on their baby girls' palms to callus them. Sometimes Clara wished she had been so lucky. There were times when walking outdoors could be overwhelming—not that noblewomen went outside often. If they wanted nature, they could visit the animal containment, the menagerie or the aquarium inside the Great Lords' Palace. The number of animals was well monitored, not like in nature, and it made her empathic abilities bearable.

Today her gown felt very heavy. The tight purple bodice was overlaid with a soft gossamer cream. Though it showed a hint of cleavage, it was a respectable amount. The skirt belled out from her hips, wider on the sides than on the front and back. As she sat, she rested her hands to her sides, elbows bent back with wrists lightly set on the skirt's sturdy frame.

The heavy weight of her wig kept her from leaning forward to watch much of what Eula did. The traveling companion was pretty and young with a husband of five years. Her husband, a stoic man of very few words, piloted their ship. Clara wanted to ask the woman if the man ever spoke in complete sentences to his wife in private, but such a question was beyond rude. People did not inquire into the state of another's marriage.

Clara felt the boot give way only to be replaced with a tiny slipper. She curled her toes, testing the strange freedom of movement as she slid her other foot forward so Eula could begin to remove the second boot. The shoes would be hidden by her skirt, but she felt it a fair compromise.

When Eula finished, Clara stood. The tent walls were a bright white, enough to let light through from the darkening outside, thick enough to hide any trace of the outdoors. Unfortunately, the floor was dirt so she was forced to walk on the extra bolts of material her mother had sent with her. They were unrolled onto the floor to create a path from her dressing room to the main part of the tent. The ceiling was low in places, dangerously close to touching her wig. As she walked along the silken path, she felt the curve of the ground beneath her feet. The slippers were strange, as if she walked barefoot, and they did little to help brace the gown's weight. Already her leg muscles began to protest the lack of support.

Her skirt brushed against the material walkway, making a light swishing noise with each step. Eula walked ahead to pull back the thick veil partitioning the private dressing area from the rest of the tent. At the same moment, the Draig king entered from the other side. She stopped, holding perfectly still. He was a kind man with an overly expressive face that she found both strange and fascinating. She wasn't used to men who smiled so readily and laughed with very little provocation. When she'd met him, he'd actually looked as if he might touch her hand. She, of course, hadn't moved to encourage such familiarity, but the fact he'd offered it with so little thought made her wonder what manner of people these Draig of the planet Qurilixen were.

She heard laughter coming from outside the tent moments before her potential husbands began to filter into the room. She saw their movements but did not look directly at them. As she moved forward to meet the king halfway across the tent, she listened to his greeting.

"Lady Clara, I hope your stay has been comfortable and the special arrangements that

have been made on your behalf are to your satis-
faction."

She glanced down to the floor to where she'd
had Eula unroll the material bolts. There was no
reason to be rude. "Yes, King Llyr. I thank you for
the hospitality." Then, turning her attention to the
man standing directly behind him, she waited
expectantly.

"My oldest son, Prince Ualan," the king said.

Ualan was a barbaric-looking man, naked but
for a fur loincloth wrapped about his waist. Clara
wasn't sure how to react to such attire. She tried
not to look at his chest, or stomach, or legs, or
shoulders and arms, but it was nearly impossible to
gaze in his direction without seeing some bit of
indecently exposed flesh. Oddly, the one place she
could look without being impolite was his face—
which he had half covered from view by a mask.
Both the king and the prince glanced at Ualan's
chest. Clara had been told how their ceremony
worked, but she half expected the glowing crystal
necklace to be a metaphor for attraction, not an
actual crystal hanging about their neck.

Ualan looked back up to her, nodded once and
said, "I wish you well in your journeys, my lady."
With that, he moved to leave the tent, allowing the
next in line to be presented to her.

That was it? No glow so no marriage? The man

hadn't even asked her a question or engaged in polite conversation. He'd just looked at her, looked at his crystal and then decided.

Clara felt a tiny thread of fear work its way into her. The next prince stepped forward, Prince Olek. He stared at her wig, not bothering to look at his chest. She eyed the crystal, willing it to have a reaction. Nothing happened. He then took his leave as quickly as his brother had.

Worry knotted her stomach. She wasn't sure what she would do if none of them wanted her. Should she have worn the traditional gown? Disgraced herself to attract them with flesh? The king had said there were eight nobles. That meant she had six left.

Prince Yusef gave her an easy smile that shone in his eyes. The look was probably meant to put her at ease, but it only made her worry more. She wondered what emotion her face gave away. As a child she'd been scolded for her expressive eyes. Did her desperation show? Did they know how badly she needed one of them to like her? To want her? She couldn't return home unmarried. Her father had made sure to point that fact out several times before her departure. Indeed, it had been the last thing he'd said to her.

As Prince Yusef stepped aside, Prince Zoran came forward. He was a man of beastly proportions whose stoic face should have brought her some comfort. Unfortunately, she couldn't get past his towering height or the thick breadth of his body to let go of her captured breath. When his crystal didn't glow, it was with relief that she watched him leave.

She was halfway through the men with no indication that any of them would change their mind and want her for a wife. She'd prepared herself for conversation or questions, but found instead the efficient soldiering of men being marched past her like an object to be inspected and disregarded.

"These are my nephews," the king said, drawing her attention to the last four men. "Lord Bronislaw, High Duke of the Draig." The man bowed his head, said something and stepped away without a glowing crystal. "Lord Aleksej, Younger Duke of Draig." Aleksej eyed her head much as Prince Olek had. Surely Eula would have told her if her hair was out of place. Aleksej's crystal also did not change.

This could not be happening. Clara knew her worth. She was pretty. She was rich. She was titled. Why didn't these barbarians see her good breeding and worth? They should all want a bride such as her. They should be trying to win her affections. She worked so hard to be perfect.

"Lord Mirek, Ealdorman of Draig." She barely

heard the king's introduction. Her mind raced and became more frantic by each passing moment. What would she do if they sent her home?

"I," she began to speak to the unimpressed Mirek, but the word was weak. She continued silently, *I can put on the gown and we can begin anew. I am a lady. I can manage a household. I am of breedable years. I come from money. Won't you consider me? Won't you let me prove my worth? Won't you marry me? I should not have been so proud. I should have married Lord Dane. Why did I think his attraction to my brother should matter? Marriage is not about emotions.*

Take me, please, my lord, or they will kill me.

The full depth of her foolishness hit her as Mirek stepped aside. How vain she had been to turn away so many suitors. Did she really think her father would wait for her to marry out of love? Did she think he would let her out of her duty should she refuse enough men?

"We have a match!" the king exclaimed, sounding surprised.

Clara blinked, pulled from her thoughts to the soft pulsating light before her. A crystal glowed. The last man was a match. She'd been so frantic, she hadn't heard his name. Her relief was short lived as a new fear worked its way into her. This meant she was staying on the primitive planet. This place was her new home. Her eyes instantly moved from the glowing crystal to the face of her future husband. He hadn't spoken, still did not speak.

She saw the brown-blond waves of his hair held down by the ties of his mask. Hazel eyes watched her intently. No one she knew had eyes that color. His mouth lifted at the corner.

Clara felt the eyes of the men on her. Her intended's expression was hidden by the mask, but she saw the intensity in his gaze. He lifted his hand as if he would touch her. Instantly, she stepped back, bowing her head to acknowledge him. Then, unsure how to react to the freely shown expressions and the growing murmur of voices, she quickly turned and went back to her dressing room.

"It seems you have been blessed, little brother," a man said. "An unusual blessing at that."

"Do not tease him," another scolded. "The will of the gods cannot be questioned. Many blessings on your house, cousin."

"Many blessings," another repeated.

Clara blocked them out, not wanting to listen. A husband. She was to be married. Finally, at last, the next generation could begin.

"And life as I know it will end," she whispered. "This cannot be happening."

"THE WILL of the gods cannot be questioned," Yusef said, quieting Mirek's teasing though he smiled as he said it. "Many blessings on your house, cousin."

"Many blessings," Ualan agreed.

"Many blessings," Olek and Alek said in unison. Their well-wishes were followed by the rest.

The men pulled their masks from their faces, all but Vlad who was near his future bride and would not risk breaking tradition by letting her see his face until she deemed it was time. He grinned. "Thank you."

"I did not think it would happen," the king said. He glanced to where the woman had disappeared and motioned the men to go outside. When they were farther from her earshot, he continued, "She is here as a favor to an old friend. Do not fear, though she does not look as we do, she is from a noble family with an impeccable reputation in the galaxy. They even sent the kingdom a rather sizeable gift for allowing her to come."

"A gift? How strange," Ualan put forth.

"To return it would be rude," the king said. "Since Vlad is to marry her, I will have the servants see to it the gift is taken to his home." Then to Vlad, he added, "It is a fine match for many reasons, nephew. You will be very blessed by the gods."

"Did you see her hair?" Alek whispered. "It's well over an arm's length above her head. Do you think her skull is shaped the same beneath?"

Vlad frowned at him. Bron slapped his brother in the chest, shutting him up.

"I'm sure it is just her custom," Mirek explained in an effort to comfort Vlad. "I have seen stranger fashions when dealing with alien species."

"Do you think our nephews will have...?" Alek gestured his hand along his temple and lifted it up high over his head to indicate the shape of Clara's presumably tall skull.

"Enough. Let us leave Vlad to his bride," Ualan said. The king nodded in agreement, motioning for the men to make their way toward the valley below. When he was alone with his nephew, he said, "Vlad, I know she does not look as we are used to women appearing, but I am sure the blue-whiteness of her skin is paint and the hair is simply a style. Her servant does not appear misshapen in such a way. Many planets have customs unlike ours. Besides, when she is your wife she will take on the customs of our home world. All will be well."

Vlad refused to comment, but he honestly did not see what everyone was so concerned about. He'd been enraptured by the clear perfection of her purple eyes. They were unlike any he'd ever seen—pure and deep. The lack of expression on her face could have been due to many things—the overwhelming reality of a new world, tiredness from a long trip, bridal nervousness. All of the concerns his family had could be fixed with a deep sleep, hot bath and reassurances of his devotion— all of which he could easily provide for her.

"I am sorry you will not be able to partake in the ceremonies, but this is a blessed day for you. I hope my sons will be so lucky." The king patted his shoulder before moving to go. "You should go with the others to give thanks for the blessing and then come back here for your bride. If she is willing, bring her to your tent below. If she will not go, stay with her here to complete the ceremony and have servants bring anything you may need. Either way, it is a blessing." The king glanced to the tent where Lady Clara remained. As dragonshifters they could hear very well, and inside the tent was silent. "On further thought, she does not appear as if she would fit in with the other brides. It may be best if she does not go down at all. I will explain my decision to the elders, that I have given permission for Lady Clara to be kept inside this specially constructed bridal tent with her new husband until the ceremony is completed in the morning. They will make allowances for you on this night and will not expect her to come down in the morning for the declaration. We will come to you before we receive the others. It will be early, so be ready."

Vlad nodded once. His uncle seemed nervous, overly explaining what to Vlad was quite a simple matter. His crystal glowed. Clara was meant to be his wife. His dreams were coming true. The rest were just details.

Vlad wanted to go to her. He wanted to peel the thick layers of her strange gown from her body to see what lay beneath. He wanted to gaze into those brilliantly colored eyes. Tonight, the wedding night, was a night of pure discovery. They would not consummate the marriage, but tradition allowed that they could do everything but. After she removed his mask, he would be free to talk to her. Before she removed the mask, he'd be free to communicate without words.

"I go to the temple," Vlad said, his voice hoarse. The sound was strange, even to his own ears.

"Many blessings," the king said, following him away from the tent.

"YOUR NOBLE FATHER WILL BE PLEASED," Eula said evenly. She smiled. It was a serene look, but Clara saw the emotion filter into the woman's eyes. "The next generation of your family can begin. You are lucky. There will be no stasis for you. You can begin your family immediately."

Clara moved a hand to her stomach. Immediately? She barely knew the barbarian and she was supposed to give him children? Of course, this was the way of things. This is what she had planned all along—a child within the first year. Her logical brain knew it. Too bad her rapidly beating heart didn't seem to understand it.

Her intended was nicely built like the others. Granted, they were the first half-naked primitives she'd ever seen, and she assumed that is what a nicely built man looked like. Everything about these people was so…unguarded.

"You are very lucky. My two younger sisters still have to find their husbands," Eula continued. She lightly touched her stomach. "I fear there may be no hope for them."

Clara blinked, looking at Eula's hand. "You're carrying?"

Eula nodded. "Yes. I go into stasis when I arrive home."

She didn't need to see the woman's expression to know she was frightened. The very fact she mentioned her pregnancy meant the upcoming sleep was on her mind. Clara hovered her hand over Eula's. "I was with my sisters. The process was very peaceful."

Eula nodded. "Of course."

"What is it?" Clara whispered.

"Husbands do not sleep."

The answer was simple, but it said much. Yet, strangely, Clara had never considered the husbands. What would it be like to go to sleep, knowing your husband was left alone? Would he find company with other women? How many years would he age? Would he be the man you knew going in to stasis? Or would decades pass and you would awake to a stranger. There was a reason they pushed generations to marry quickly so that didn't happen, but Clara was proof that siblings did not always cooperate. Seeing Eula's expression caused her a degree of guilt she hadn't felt before.

"Do you require that I stay?" Eula asked.

Clara shook her head in denial. "No. This is where I belong. Your husband will be waiting to fly you back. I will interrupt your life no more."

Eula nodded. "Would you like me to deliver a message to your lady mother?"

"Tell her I have done my duty. Tell her the next generation can begin." Clara wanted to say more. She wanted to be home. She wanted to beg her mother to send for her, to not abandon her here. She wanted to see the thin veins in her mother's wrist, the brief show of affection allowed her. None of those things would happen. Eula would leave and Clara would be left alone on this planet.

"Your message will be delivered," Eula said. "Honor to your union, Lady Clara."

"Honor to your family," Clara answered as the woman left.

Alone in the tent, Clara simply stood in the middle of the room. She focused on her breathing, counting the seconds as they passed. When she lost count, she simply started again. It was an old trick, one she'd started as a young girl to keep calm. She imagined she heard her ship take off. She counted faster.

Twelve, thirteen, four, five, six…

"My lady?"

Clara froze.

"My lady?"

She hesitated before moving out of her dressing area toward the man who spoke. Before seeing him, she knew it was her husband. Clara paused in the entryway.

The man still wore the mask over the upper half of his face. The tent seemed smaller than before, as if the walls had been pushed in when she had not been paying attention.

He smiled at her. "Come."

Clara did as he commanded, moving toward

him. She didn't speak as she lifted her hands. She touched as little of him as possible as she hooked the tips of her longer thumbnails along the side straps of the mask. She knew what was expected of her and she did her duty like a good bride. She pulled the mask up and off his head. Hazel eyes met hers. His smile widened.

"I am very pleased, bride," he said.

Clara let the mask dangle on her thumbnail and offered it to him. He took it without question. He studied her face expectantly. Only she wasn't sure what he expected.

"I believe that is all of the ceremony until tomorrow," Clara stated.

"We can speak if you like," the man said. "Or…"

She continued to look at him, doing her best to ignore the pounding of her heart and her trembling hands. Calm. She must be calm. There was comfort in that cultural demand. "Speak."

"Yes." He nodded. The man had a proud face, a fine face, even if his expressions were open, flooding her empathic senses with their emotions. She found herself both fascinated and disturbed at the same time.

"Speak of what?"

"Anything. You must be curious about your new home." He glanced around and then tossed the mask aside to the floor. It landed in the dirt, off the material path she now stood on. There was nothing inside this section of the tent. She had been told that was because it was a temporary stopping place where she could get ready for the ceremony.

"Of course." She nodded once.

Moments passed in silence. He looked as if he would reach for her. "I live in the mountains to the north. Perhaps you saw them when you arrived?"

"I was not allowed to look out onto the planet," Clara explained, wondering if the question was a test to see if she really was a noblewoman. "Only the pilot is allowed in the cockpit. It is no place for ladies."

"Do you enjoy the outdoors?" The man kept staring at her. She wished he'd look away, or at least not appear so interested.

Clara moved her gaze down. "I enjoy looking at the out of doors very much. There is a large viewing screen in my… Forgive me. I amend with a correction. There *was* a large viewing screen in my chambers in my former home."

"Viewing screen?" he repeated. His smile fell some.

"Yes." She tried not to stare at him, but it was difficult. She found her eyes moving to study him as he did her.

"Do you go out of doors?" he asked.

What a strange question. "I left my home to go onto the ship. I have been through many doors. It is the custom of my people to use entryways when coming and going."

His lips twitched up a little at the side. "What do you enjoy?"

"I," Clara hesitated. No one had ever in her entire life asked her such a thing. She was unsure how to answer. "I read. Things."

"Books?"

She nodded once.

"Anything else?"

"I…" She wasn't sure what would be proper. She liked to daydream, but that was not honorable. She sometimes made up stories in her head. She liked to dance when no one was watching. She hummed to herself when no one was listening.

Apparently, she took too long to give him an answer, because he continued, "I enjoy running, hiking in the mountains, sleeping outdoors, riding ceffyls, weapons training…" He grinned, the look coming to his face as if spontaneously. "I try to carve stones, though I cannot say I am the most talented at it. The village children seem to like them well enough to play with them though."

"I…" She again hesitated. "I do none of those things."

He looked as if he wanted to say more but had

run out of words. "Perhaps I should have the servants bring up food and supplies to make your night in this tent more comfortable." He began to turn, only to stop. "Unless you will be too uncomfortable with our custom of spending this night in a tent? I assure you that you will be safe. We are by the royal palace, surrounded by palace guards."

"It is your custom. I have been prepared to honor it," she said, though it was thoughtful of him to think of her comfort. Perhaps there was some hope for him.

"Very well. I will return."

"A moment, my lord," she said as he reached for the tent flap. He glanced back at her and she added, "I do have one question."

"Yes?"

"Your name? I would like to know my husband's name." She tried not to let her eyes trail down his strong back.

At that, he laughed. "I am Lord Vladan, Ealdorman Honorary of Draig."

"That is your full title?"

"Yes. I am also the High Mining Official." He again reached for the tent flap. "But you may address me as Vlad. There is no reason for formality between husband and wife."

"I am Lady Clara of the Redding," she offered. "My name is Lady Clara."

"I know, Lady Clara," he said softly. He dropped the flap as if deciding not to leave and moved toward her. She stiffened as he neared but did not back away. He lifted his hand to her face. That first touch was so gentle, so soft. She could barely feel it but for the heat jumping off his flesh onto hers. "You are very beautiful, Clara. I am very pleased to call you my wife. All that I have is yours. It is my hope you will come to love your new home."

"I am bound by duty to love it," she answered logically.

"I will respect that answer," he whispered. Was it her imagination or did he lean closer? "For now."

Clara didn't move. Vlad brushed his mouth against hers. An electric shock of awareness zapped through her. She stopped breathing even as her heart exploded wildly in her chest. It only lasted a brief second, but she could still feel him as he withdrew.

"I will order food brought to you and a bath, should you desire one. I am told you have a bed." He gestured to her dressing room. She nodded. "Very good. I will be back, beautiful Clara."

Clara watched him go, only moving to touch her mouth when she was alone. A low hum left her, half song, half exclamation of what she was feeling deep inside. "Very good," she whispered.

3

CLARA STARED at the steaming hot bathwater in the metal tub. Several large servants, all men, had brought the bath to the tent. She felt their eyes on her, studying her as the people on her home world studied a painting in the Palace Noblae Portraite Gallery. They hauled the tub with long, thin wood handles that easily detached after they lowered it to the ground. Others brought a table, others food, others furs to cover the dirt floor and still others pitchers of wine. There was really too much food for two people to eat on their own.

"Will others be joining us?" Clara asked, still looking at the tub. She'd read about water baths, but on her home world they used laser cleaning systems. Learning to swim was a prerequisite in her household, so she had felt water before but had not used it to clean herself.

"You wish for me to call the servants back to bathe you?" Vlad asked. "That won't be necessary. Should you need help, I will bathe you."

Shocked, she turned her rounded eyes to him. Her mouth opened, but no sound came out. It took her a full three seconds to gain her composure. She forced her expression to settle. "I was speaking of the food. There is much of it."

"Ah." He gave a small laugh. "It is a night of feasting. They wished to make sure you were well satisfied."

She eyed the towering plates of cooked meat, three loaves of blue bread, crusted pastries and the assortment of fruits and creamed substances. "There is too much. I could not eat so much in a lifetime. Since it has been prepared, we should order that it be given to the poor so that all may eat tonight."

He went to the table and lifted a small, round fruit and tossed it into his mouth. "All may eat every night."

"I speak of the poor who cannot afford to feed themselves," she explained.

His smile widened. "We have no such poor. All here are prosperous. No one is left wanting for food or clothing or shelter."

"How is such a thing possible? I have never been to a place that did not have their poor." She took a small step closer to him. "You are rich, so you must have poor. If you do not associate directly with them, I am sure the servants will know where they reside."

"It is not so remarkable that we don't have poverty. Everyone is expected to pull their own weight the best they can. Those who cannot are provided for. If children are left without family, they are taken in to another's home to be raised." He ate another piece of fruit before lifting a third in offering to her.

"People will take in the children of others?" she questioned. "They are not made to serve in the new family's home?"

His hand dropped. "Your people make orphaned children serve?"

She nodded. "We try to put them in the same household so that they may be together."

He set the fruit down on the plate and did not lift another. "It is not the fault of the child that their circumstances have changed. If parents die, they should not be forced into servitude."

"If the parents have not provided for them, it cannot be expected that another take on their expense," she answered. Clara wondered what kind of person would be willing to take in twelve to thirty displaced children upon their parents' deaths into a household already filled with just as many. It would be a huge burden for most families to raise over fifty children.

"Our people clearly have different views on the matter," he said.

"I would assume we will have different views on many things."

At her words, his eyes traveled up to her wig. He nodded. "And styles."

She lifted her hand but did not touch her hair. "I must appear strange to you. When I met your queen, she did not look as I do."

The Draig queen had a wild appeal to her, with natural flowing hair and a very simplistic tunic gown that formed to the woman's body without seeming to constrict it as Clara's gown did. At first, Clara had thought Queen Mede was a servant.

The man nodded. "Strange, yes. Beautiful, yes."

"And my skin." She looked at her hand, seeing the pale blue-white paint.

"Strange, yes." He approached and took her by the fingers to lift her hand. His warm thumb rubbed against the back of her wrist, as if to remove the coloring.

Clara's entire body jolted to life at the touch. As

a lady, her hands hardly made contact with anything, let alone another person's flesh. The strange texture of his skin to hers caused every thought inside her stunned brain to stop. She stretched her fingers wide, trying not to return the contact. Each nerve fired at once, as if the appendage would jump off her arm and run into hiding. Yet she couldn't pull away from him as she should. The sensations were too much for her to process. Flashes of talons warred with visions of running wild in the forest. This man carried an animal inside him. She wasn't frightened so much as fascinated.

"But very beautiful," Vlad continued before his voice slipped into the Qurilixian language. He kept talking and she could no longer understand his words. It was a smoothly spoken, soft tonal language with harder guttural edges seamlessly woven in.

"The universal translator I had implanted does not speak your language and I only know my ancestors' language and the universal star language." She watched his fingers on her flesh, mesmerized by their soft movements and the intimacy of their touch.

"It was something my father used to say to my mother," he answered. She waited, but he didn't translate it for her.

"You lost your father?" she asked, feeling it was so.

"And my mother," he answered. "My father was trapped in a mine collapse, and my mother went in to save him. They did not come back out. And your parents?"

"They are very pleased to have me, their last daughter, married." Clara tried not to think of the celebrations she would miss—of her sisters waking and giving birth, of the next generation beginning.

"You have siblings?"

They were whispering. He stood close and still touched her hand. She was unused to the intimacy of shared body heat, yet she couldn't bring herself to pull away. There was something to the sound of his voice and the feel of his touch. "Yes. There are thirty-three in the house of Redding. Nineteen sisters, eleven brothers, myself and my parents. I am the last to marry."

"And I thought we had large families." Vlad chuckled. "Most families here have four to eight sons."

"And how many daughters?" she asked.

"No daughters." His grip tightened on her hand. Clara only noticed because she was so focused on the feel of his fingers.

"You…?" She stiffened, almost afraid to receive

an answer to her fear. "Do you dispose of the girls as a burden?"

"No. We simply do not produce many female offspring. One of the very last Qurilixian females born was the queen. Scientists have looked into it and decided the blue radiation from our suns, while making us thrive, also prevents the birth of females except for the rare occurrence. Thousands of males may be born before a female is conceived."

"Were those other men your brothers?" She tugged lightly at her hand, trying to block the empathic connection so she could better focus on what she was saying.

"The princes are my cousins. Alek, Mirek and Bron are my brothers."

"I see. They appear very—" she tried to think of a way to describe them, "—open."

He laughed. She realized he did that a lot, though she did not understand what could be so amusing as to warrant the sound.

"My sisters are Elisa, Louisa, Evita, Clavia, Mandia, Maria, Jacia, Lydia, Saria, Noria, Doria, Coria, Horia, Valora, Honara, Honora, Dara, Daria and Laney." Clara paused. She knew that there were way too many names for him to remember, but she did not want the conversation to end. If it did, he might let go of her hand, and she wasn't done experiencing his touch. "My brothers are Alban, Emeric, Edgard, Firmin, Florenten, Gael, Bael, Gaubert, Gaspard, Herve and Ignace."

"And Clara," he said. Vlad's fingers trailed up her hand to her wrist. "Beautiful Clara."

Vlad let go of her hand. The connection snapped into nothingness. She didn't lower her arm right away. Coolness replaced his warmth. He reached up and touched her wig. Her eyes shot up, but it was too late to protest as he lifted it from her head. The pins snagged her hair and she gasped. "Ow."

He set it back down. "I did not mean to injure you. How do you remove it?"

Her hands shaking, Clara pulled a pin and then another with the tips of her fingers, unfastening the wig. When it loosened its hold, he lifted it again. With the heavy weight gone, her head felt dizzy. She closed her eyes until the lightheaded sensation passed. Vlad set the wig on the table next to the food. Clara touched her head with her wrist. The netting holding her natural locks to her head remained. She rubbed it gingerly. Only her maids had looked at her without her wig since she'd come into womanhood. Not meeting his eyes, she worked the netting off her scalp with her thumbnail. Instantly, four braids of her hair fell around her shoulders, two in front, two in back. The braids acted as a support for the wig. The blonde locks reached her waist when untwined, but now fell to mid back.

"I thought your hair might be darker," he said thoughtfully, looking at her eyebrows. She'd darkened them with purple kohl.

"I do not always wear the body paint. It is our custom for special occasions. If I had not dressed in such a way, it would have been considered an insult by my people. My father would not have been pleased with the reports." What was it about this man that made her so self-conscious? They were alien to each other. She didn't expect they would understand each other's ways nor have the same styles and customs. Though when she'd thought to marry a nobleman, she hadn't expected such differences. She was all too aware of his half-naked state. There was little to separate them from touching.

When he moved, she found she enjoyed watching his muscles beneath his flesh. Even his neck was strong. Men where she came from were…softer.

"So this dress is like our traditional bridal gown? It is only worn this one night?" he asked.

"My gown?" Clara looked at her dress. "It is new, but I thought I might wear it again. If you do not like it, I have others. I assure you I came with a full trousseau."

"Trousseau?"

"Bridal chest. As I am female, my family provides everything I might need to start my marriage so that the burden does not fall upon my new husband." She again looked at the gown. It was the finest quality. In fact, it was her best one. "I should thank you for allowing your crystal to glow."

"Thank me?" He glanced down at the stone that still illuminated his chest with a soft light. "I had nothing to do with the glowing. It is fate, the will of the gods shown to us. You were meant to be my wife, that is all."

The comment stayed with her as she turned her back to him. She touched a braid, pulling at the end of it. For a moment, she'd allowed herself to think that he'd chosen to be with her—quickly, yes, but still chosen. He said a force had chosen *for* him —gods, parents, emperor, it didn't matter. An arranged marriage was an arranged marriage. She suppressed the hope that had filled her upon their meeting. This marriage was a duty, an arrange-ment. She would do her duty. She would bare her children and then she would go home to live her days alone.

"Are you finished speaking to me?" she asked. "It has been a long journey and I would sleep before tomorrow's ceremony is concluded."

"Of course," he answered. "Would you care to eat first?"

"No, thank you," she said, not very hungry. With Eula gone she felt very alone. The only traces she had of her life were waiting for her behind the thin material leading to her dressing chamber. She wanted to surround herself with them, meager as the belongings were. Sadness filled her. Quietly, she said, "To a good night, Lord Vlad."

VLAD WATCHED his bride move into the private dressing area and frowned. She was going to sleep? On this night? So early?

Yes, their conversation had been a little stunted. Her expressions and the tone of her voice were very hard to interpret. Though he was sure he would learn the nuances of reading her in time. She had expressive purple eyes. He noticed the widening of her pupils when she talked of her home and family. It was a tiny shift, but it was there.

He looked at the wig. Such a strange thing, so alien in nature. It created a dome over the head, tall and towering, adding an almost ridiculous amount of height. When he'd lifted it from her, it had been surprisingly heavy. Vlad glanced at where she'd disappeared and picked the wig up. Curious, he set it briefly on his head. The experiment lasted all of four seconds before he took it off and set it back on the table. It was like carrying a small child atop his brain. The hairpiece would be the first thing to go. He would not have his wife tortured.

Clara's gown also appeared to be weighted down with tiny gemstones. He could tell by the way the material moved and by her deliberate steps as she walked. Why would a woman choose to torture herself thus? Strange, strange aliens. He made a mental note to buy her a new wardrobe immediately. His wife would not be brutalized by her clothing. Besides, the cumbersome dress would hamper him when he seduced his beautiful bride after the ceremony was complete.

He closed his eyes and let a partial shift wash over him. Being a dragon-shifter was not something they publicized. The Draig preferred their privacy, and the less the outside universe knew about them the better. Lack of knowledge was a powerful deterrent to those who would think to harm them and an advantage if an off-world enemy ever tried to attack.

The smell of her lingered in the room. What a strange alien scent, the perfume she wore enhancing the subtler smell of her skin. With his superior senses, he could detect it easily.

He listened, finding the gentle sound of her breathing behind the thin veil of a door. Though steady and deep, it came a bit too fast. It was punc-tuated by a light scraping sound, even-tempoed and repetitive. Nails against flesh? Perhaps against her palm? A nervous gesture?

Vlad wanted to go to her. This was not how a wedding night should be. Instead, he went to the table and forced himself to eat. It was possible things were as she said. She'd had a long journey and was tired. He would have to force himself to be patient. They had a lifetime to get to know each other. The gods would not have chosen her for him if it was not fated. He trusted destiny and respected the gods. Lady Clara was meant to be his bride and they would live their days happy. End of story.

GET pregnant and then I can go home to my family, Clara thought, digging her fingernails into the flesh of her palm. It was an old habit, one she'd had since childhood. She only did it when she needed to redirect an overabundance of emotions...or in this case, erase the feel of Vlad against her skin. Undoubtedly, Eula would report the kind of primi-tive place Lady Clara had been exiled to. Then, when Clara arrived home carrying a child—a male child if the Draig genetics were to be believed—surely her father and mother would allow her to

live out her days in their home. The next generation would begin and she would be a marvelous
aunt to her sibling's children. And her one child
would grow around much family. She just wouldn't
tell them about the male-dominated genetics of the
Draig, or else her father might change five to
twenty in hopes of getting more grandsons—primitive genetics or not. Then there was the idea that
an animal of some kind resided in her husband. A
shifter? She had not been told these men were
shifters. Her parents would be most surprised to
discover it. Out of all the females in her family, she
was the most sensitive to animals. The idea of one
residing in her husband didn't frighten her as it
would her delicate sisters.

Only one child? The idea of a lone child with
no siblings was sad. She did not want to be the
breeder her mother was, but one seemed like a very
lonely number. She could not imagine her childhood without the constant activity of her siblings.

Vlad would satisfy his people's tradition of the
glowing crystal by taking her as a bride. When she
left, he would be free to take lovers. At the very
logical course of her thoughts, she frowned. For
some reason, the idea of her husband taking lovers
made her uneasy. Sure, that was the way of things.
Men took lovers, sometimes many. What else were
they supposed to do when their wives were in stasis,

or pregnant, or recovering from delivery? Such was common knowledge, and Clara hadn't really stopped to think about it too hard until Eula mentioned her own worries. Besides, the women of the planet Redde had a grand way of dealing with such knowledge—they pretended it didn't exist.

Clara did not like so much pretending.

She closed her eyes, forcing steady, deep breaths. It was time to grow up and put away her girlhood fancies. She was beginning an arranged marriage. Fate and love had nothing to do with it. Soon she would go home to live out her life as a matronly aunt and mother of one. She convinced herself Eula's report would carry weight with her parents, who would surely be stunned at the true level of barbarity their last married daughter was to endure. The companion would tell them how she had unrolled the expensive material to cover the dirt floor. And then there was the appalling lack of material on the wedding gown they had wanted her to wear. Well, perhaps Eula wouldn't tell her mother that part. The conversation would be positively too indecent for a maid to share with a lady. Furthermore, Clara was being made to sleep in a tent where anyone with a knife could slip through the thin walls, though for some reason that was the least of Clara's worries this night. Even she could admit she felt a sense of safety.

Who would want to kill a bride on her wedding night?

Slowly, her heart calmed and the scratching of her nails erased the intimacy of Vlad's touch with the pain of sore flesh, at least enough that she could concentrate past the memory of it. All would be well. This detour to the planet Qurilixen was simply a small part of her life's story.

4

SLEEP WOULD NOT COME, and Clara found herself scratching at the paint on her arms, trying to dig the true color of her flesh from beneath the sheen of bluish white. There was a bath waiting in the other room of the tent, though the water was most likely cold by now. Outside, evening darkened the sky. Inside, the only way she could see was from the torchlight flickering near the edges of the tent. The fire was arranged in such a way that it didn't burn the enclosure. The tent was quiet. Vlad had most likely left to join the festivities.

Without Eula, it had been hard to remove her heavy gown herself, and the idea of trying to put it back on caused her tired muscles to scream in protest. She took her robe and slid the soft material over her arms and wrapped the extended bottom flap around her waist several times before fastening it into place. Her steps were short because of the robe's tighter skirt. She pulled the tent flap aside, seeing first the table towering with food.

In preparation of the day, she had not dined as she was accustomed. With that thought in mind, she went to the food, studying the massive spread. At home, the female diet was very strict. Each meal amounted to about half the size of her hand. Only men were given larger portions. She reached slowly for a piece of fruit.

"You may have all that you like."

She gasped, quickly looking around the tent for Vlad. It took a moment to find him, but when she did she saw he had helped himself to the bath. A goblet of wine sat on the floor next to a pitcher, easily within reach of his hand. Fingers tapped lightly against the side of the tub.

Her gaze followed his arm up a strong shoulder and corded neck. He watched her with intensity. Moisture beaded on his face and slicked back his hair. A tiny rivulet trailed down his cheek, disappearing into the dark shadow beneath his jaw. The soft glow of the crystal was muted by the water, but she saw it beneath the surface.

"I thought I was alone," she said, not reaching for the food. Clara wondered if she should offer him privacy, but it was not unusual on her home world for wives to help bathe husbands, and he seemed perfectly at ease with his circumstance.

"It would please me greatly if you ate something. If what is offered does not tempt you, I will send servants for more." He watched expectantly. She didn't move. "I will order different foods brought until you eat. At some point they will suspect you are purposefully refusing the hospitality of our planet." He gave a small smile, as if he knew he was manipulating her.

The manipulation worked. Feeling guilty for not accepting the generosity of her new home, she took the piece of fruit and ate it. None of the food was cut into small pieces for her so she was forced to take the smallest option. The tiny morsel was incredibly sweet, almost too much so.

Vlad's smile widened as she chewed. "Thank you, my lady. I would hate for you to wither away."

Taking a knife from one of the platters, she cut a thin slice of the blue bread, set it on the trencher and cut it into small size cubes. They were uneven as she was unused to holding knives in her hand. She tried the bread. Despite the strange color, it tasted very much like the grains on her planet. She finished the bread, well aware of his eyes watching her.

"Thank you," she said, stepping away from the food.

"You may have more."

She shook her head in denial. "I had a lady's portion. I am fine." Before he could comment further on her eating habits, she turned her attention to the dark tent wall. Anything was better than staring at the droplets of water clinging to his jaw. "I thought there were festivities on this night of darkness."

"There are," he said, "in the valley below."

"You do not wish to join the others?"

"My festivities are here." The softness of his tone made her shiver.

"You do not have to remain here for my benefit." Clara wondered what a Draig festival might look like. She imagined them to be a rambunctious affair. Even as she wanted to see it, she did not wish to participate. She wanted to peek in from a safe distance and merely observe it. Too bad her mother had not sent a portable viewing screen for her to use—not that she would have been able to pick up any signals in the tent.

She heard movement behind her. Water stirred and dripped. How could she resist one quick look?

Clara turned back to him. He was her husband. She should be free to look if he chose to show her. Already the Draig custom of walking about half-clothed was very apparent. Instantly, her eyes were drawn to the crystal. It bounced against his chest as he lifted a foot from the water. The wet stone pointed downward, drawing attention to the illuminated breadth of his chest and the tapering of his lean waist.

Clara wasn't so sheltered as to not know the difference between men and women, yet seeing that difference in very real, very naked glory was something else altogether. His member lay nestled between his thighs only to shift and move as he reached for a white square of material stacked nearby. He bent over to grab the cloth, giving her a full view of his backside. She had the strangest urge to touch him—it warred with the urge to quickly avert her eyes, which was overcome by the desire to continue watching.

When he stood, his eyes met hers. He gave her a knowing grin. Vlad clearly knew she watched and he didn't care.

"You look nice with your hair down." Vlad blotted his skin before moving to tie the white material around his waist.

Clara touched her locks. She'd brushed them out but had yet to re-braid. Her attention was drawn to her blue hand. "If it is not too much trouble, I would like to bathe."

He gestured behind his bathing tub. "I had another brought for you."

She moved closer to see where he indicated. There was a second bath.

Vlad drew his hands through his wet hair, slicking it back and wringing the excess water from it. He tilted his head to the side. Droplets rained behind him on the ground. His eyes narrowed and he lifted a finger to her chin, slid a thumb over her jaw in a light caress. "Would you like me to bathe you?"

"Bathe me?" she asked in surprise. He'd shocked her with that very same offer earlier. "That will not be necessary. I have no wish to reduce you to be my handmaid."

At that, he laughed. It was a deep, rich, highly amused sound. He dropped his hand. "And I can assure you, my lady, I have no wish to be a hand-maid. Such a position was not what I had in mind."

"You plan something?" she asked for clarification. Her voice was not as strong as she would've liked, but for some reason she could barely catch her breath. Perhaps she had tied the flap of her robe too tight against her waist. She followed the movements of his hand against her face.

"This night is about discovery. I had thought to let you sleep, but since you are now awake I would like to continue with the custom." He took a step closer, towering over her. His chest was near her face. She looked at the crystal, watching the pulsing light grow in intensity. It was as if she felt the pulsating rhythm inside her, slow and steady, unfurling in her lower stomach. "I would very much like to bathe you, my lady."

"As a lady, I cannot allow that," she answered.

"What about as a woman?" He dipped his head close to her ear. He didn't touch her, but she felt his heat against her clothing and his breath against her neck.

"As a lady, I cannot allow that," she whispered, not really thinking about what she said.

"Pity." The soft tickle of his breath mesmerized her senses. Men did not get this close on her world. Well, one suitor had tried, but her father had thrown him from the estate and fined him a thousand space credits for the presumption.

"I have been instructed, if you wish to begin the next generation." Clara had no idea a man's nearness could make her all fluttery inside.

He laughed again. Clara stiffened, drawing physically back. She had not expected her offer to meet with such a response.

"I have never heard the marriage act referred to in such," he paused, still grinning, "terms."

"Thank you for the meal, my lord. I will now retire." Clara forced herself to walk with dignity toward her dressing area.

"No, bride." Vlad grabbed her wrist to stop her,

instead directing her toward him. "Do not look so vexed with me. Your words simply took me by surprise. When I look at you, it is not with thoughts of beginning a new generation."

"Oh." Clara pulled her hand back. She lightly rubbed her flesh where he'd touched her. The pulsing crystal caught her notice, drawing her attention toward it. Monitoring her expression, she focused on projecting a serene image.

The blue paint probably did look strange to him. No wonder he was not thinking of taking her to bed. Then a terrible thought occurred to her. She was assured she made for a pretty woman. What if he was one of those men who preferred the company of other men? Such things were not unheard of. Lord Dane was proof of that. In fact, no one really cared if men took male lovers so long as they did their duty by their wives. Would Vlad do his duty by her and get her pregnant so that she could return home?

"I understand now," she answered. "If you do not mind, I would like to bathe. Please, join the festivities if you like."

"I cannot leave the tent. It is tradition."

She nodded. Her hand went to her waist. Even if he wasn't interested in looking at her, she still felt uneasy about allowing him to see. Yes, eventually he would watch her undress—as her husband—but it would not be tonight. Clara eyed him expectantly. He still wore the cloth around his waist and made no move to turn from her.

"Is it also tradition that you inspect me before the ceremony is complete? I assure you my race is compatible. I would not have been allowed to come otherwise."

"It is tradition." His voice sounded strained. Perhaps this was not pleasant for him.

"Very well, if it is tradition." She turned her back to him and reached for her waist to begin unwinding the material. Her fingers shook, but she did not let any personal insecurity stop her from doing what she must. That was not the kind of lady she had been raised to be.

Clara slipped the robe from her shoulders and neatly folded the soft material over her arm. The thin material of her dressing gown offered little protection. She only now became aware of how very little. When she looked behind her, his eyes were on her, intensely watching. They made her nervous. Nothing about this man's expressions was familiar. They burned with fire and struck with humor. They were open, yet unreadable. What was she to think when there was so much inside his gaze? She was used to the controlled, dispassionate expressions of her people. Things that need to be said were said with words, or they were just understood.

"Allow me to take that for you, my lady," he said, quickly moving forward to attain her robe. She forced her fingers to release it. Without it to cover her front side, she found she wasn't sure what to do with her hands. She thought about lifting them to cover her chest, to hide the fact that the thin material would reveal the color of her nipples to him. Or perhaps she should cross her hands before her hips, to disguise the light thatch of hair between her thighs. She opted to cross her wrists in front of her.

"As you can see, I am compatible." Why was she stalling? She knew he expected to examine her. It wasn't like her not to perform a duty.

"I can see little." His tone was low, soft, dark. She couldn't meet his gaze.

"Of course." She had expected him to say as much. Though, as she reached to take off her gown, she found herself wishing he would feel at least something toward her. Even if he did not think of her in sexual terms, perhaps there could be some interest in her form, something, anything.

Once her hands started their task, they did not stop. She pinched the gown, pulled it over her head and draped it over her arm to keep it from falling on the ground. Instantly, he was there to take it from her. He set her clothing aside, placing them atop the wig on the table. Clara didn't move, couldn't move. She kept her eyes forward, her chin lifted. She didn't dare look at his face, not yet. She was too afraid of what she would read in his expression. If it was disappointment or indifference, she would not be able to keep her feelings to herself. These people were so expressive, she was sure she would read such emotions easily. At least at home it was not always easy to tell what someone was thinking. Private thoughts stayed private. Here, she wasn't sure there was such a thing as a private thought.

By all the gods, his wife was a true goddess.

Vlad could barely move. He held back, out of her eye line as he tried to get some semblance of control over his rampant desire. He knew this was going to be a difficult night, but he had no idea just how very torturous. His bride was the very definition of perfection.

Her long blonde hair fell over her back and shoulders. It teased him, showing just a hint of her breasts through the locks. The curve of her hips and ass naturally drew his attention. He gripped his hands into tight fists. When she'd worn the gown the bluish paint had covered her flesh, but like this he could see the creaminess of her complexion.

Her legs were strong. If he had to guess it was from hauling around the impossible weight of that gown she'd been wearing. Yet, despite the strength, she looked soft.

Vlad wanted desperately to test the suppleness of her skin for himself. Where she was yielding, he was hard. The idea that she was made to mold against him caused a very stiff, very potent reaction in his loins. Wet, soft, soft, wet. He closed his eyes briefly and nearly lost himself beneath the drying linen clinging to his waist.

Clara didn't move and he didn't stop looking. His hands began to shift, talons growing from his fingertips to dig into his palms. He felt the tingling insistence of the beast inside him. If he couldn't lay claim to her like the human inside him wanted, the dragon wanted to surge forth to ease the desire. The Draig could not claim women in shifted form, and sometimes shifting was the only way to ease the longing of their intense sexual appetites.

Oh, but he did not want to ease the pain, not yet. He wanted to feel it, to look at her, to suffer in the sweet torture of what her body was doing to him. He forced the dragon back inside.

Perhaps he could touch her, just a little. Breathing hard, he moved behind her. His hand shook, but the scent of her was in his head—so sweet, so erotic—calling to him. With little thought as to what he was doing, he straightened his fingers and slid them between her thighs from behind. Instantly, she gasped and tensed. He watched her ass, seeing his hand buried between her legs. He slid the fingers upward, toward her sex. Heat radiated there.

Vlad closed his eyes and bowed his head. He focused on her softness, on her scent filling his nostrils. Her hair smelled exotic, like an alien flower he had never seen. The side of his finger bumped into her sex. Already she was wet. Her folds parted easily for him. He eased his hand higher, not stopping to think of his actions.

Clara's body rocked lightly. Vlad pulled at his waist, releasing the drying linen. With his free hand, he took his erection and began to stroke, just as his hand started to rub his bride. She made a light gasping noise as he moved. The sound only propelled him on. His hand firmly gripped his shaft, stroking harder and faster. Blast, he wanted to be inside her. He turned his hand, forcing her legs to accommodate the change in position. When her legs spread just enough, he slid a finger up into her. Sweet, wet heat enveloped him.

By all the gods, it was too much.

Vlad removed his hand and quickly snaked it

around her waist. He pulled her back against his hip while delving his hand between her thighs. This time, he stroked her from the front. He buried his lips against her neck, kissing her flesh through the tangles of her hair. When he opened his eyes, his shifted gaze made out the delicate texture of her skin. He looked over her shoulder, down her chest to two very ripe, perfect breasts. The nipples were hard without being touched, and he promised himself that he would taste them very soon.

Her ass pressed to his hip, the cleft flush against his flesh. He stayed against her as he turned just enough so his cock was near her hip while keeping her butt against him. He delved his finger inside her while his palm brushed along her clit.

He wanted to thrust himself inside her, but knew he could not—not yet, not on this night. So instead he opened the hand on his cock and pressed the hard shaft against her flesh while rubbing himself with the flat of his palm. Her hips jerked, as if instinctively starting their own approving rhythm. Her moisture flooded his hand. He bit at her neck gently, sucking and licking and kissing her through her hair. Oh, and those breasts, so close, begging him to touch them but just out of his mouth's reach.

A low growl sounded in the back of his throat. "Touch your breasts."

Her hands didn't move.

"Touch your breasts," he repeated into her ear before biting at the lobe. "Both hands."

She lifted her hands and covered her breasts with her palms. He groaned at the sight of her delicate fingers, imagining what they would feel like cupping him. It was by sheer desire and willpower that he stayed braced upright as she leaned into him for support.

Vlad groaned. He swung her around to face the table, letting go of her sex long enough to push her over. She leaned with her forearms flat to the wood. Then, coming behind her, he pressed his cock against her ass, letting the cheeks caress him as he rocked against her. With his hands free, he licked the taste of her off his fingers before pressing the wet digits back to her sex. The other he used to explore her breasts and lock her tight to him.

It was easy to imagine he was taking her fully. With each thrust of his hips, her clit was forced hard against his fingers. He rolled a budded nipple between his thumb and forefinger.

"Sweet goddess," he whispered. "My sweet, sweet temptress."

Her body tensed and shook ever so gently. She was close. He could feel it. The tip of his crystal bumped against her back as he leaned over her. It caught his attention, reminding him that this woman was his, fully and completely.

Clara trembled again, this time jerking harder. She made a soft sound, so soft he would have missed it if he had not been so focused on her reaction. Vlad couldn't hold back. He exploded, losing himself against her ass. The warm release slickened them as he slid easily a few more times.

"Mm," he hummed in approval. He didn't let go of her right away. Instead, he kept his hand on her sex and his cock buried along the cleft of her ass. Too bad he couldn't have penetrated her, but he had no complaints. "You are very sweet, bride."

Sweet?

The word stuck with her long after Vlad pulled his body away from her. When her senses recovered, she'd been very glad that he could not see her face. For the life of her, she couldn't remember if she'd kept her composure. All she recalled was the bombardment of feelings—tingling, pulling, wetness, friction, burning, pulsing, needing, pleasure, confusion, fear, panic, cellular explosion, and then his hands, his breath, his smell, his body erupting in wet finale.

Clara hoped she had not embarrassed herself.

It was just his touch was so...unexpected. She didn't know how else to describe it. At first, she'd thought he simply meant to ensure their compatibility. Such inspection made sense. It would not do for them to marry only to find out they were not physically compatible. And, since she was clearly not the one to determine such things, it made sense that he would do the inspection. As her husband, he would have full access to her body.

The thought caused her to shiver as she sunk lower into the warmth of the tub. The water had been clear until she washed the blue from her skin. Leaning her head against the rim, she closed her eyes. She instantly saw the appeal of soaking in water. It was much more relaxing than cleaning lasers. The pressure of the water cocooned her, wrapping her like a warm, wet blanket.

"Clara?" The sound was far away. "Clara!"

She jerked when she felt hands touching her naked arms. She flailed in the tub, pushing up with her feet. Blinking heavily, she looked at Vlad.

"You cannot fall asleep in there," he said. "Come on, let's get you to the bed."

Her dry hair stuck to her back as he lifted her out of the bath. She had pulled the long length up so it wouldn't get wet but a few tendrils had come loose. Her father had insisted they learn to swim as children, and she knew from experience that if she got her hair wet, it would take an entire day for it to fully dry. She had a travel laser comb that would take care of cleaning the locks.

Clara closed her eyes, leaning her head against his shoulder. He smelled of the same soap he'd given her to use. Yet somehow on him it smelled different, better.

She heard him whisper, felt the soft cushion as he laid her down. She did not open her eyes. All the worry and stress building up to this ceremony had left her tired now that it was done. She was married. The next generation could begin. There was nothing more for her to do this night.

VLAD WANTED to crawl into bed next to his bride but didn't want to risk waking her. The other impulse, to stand over her, staring at her beautiful naked body did hold some appeal, but he decided it would be best to leave her be. She'd self-admittedly had a long journey to get to his home world, and he'd already pushed things a little too far with his actions.

But how could he help himself? She was too much to resist. She was his fate, his destiny, his wife.

Even so, he thought it best to keep their almost joining a secret—not that he was one to brag about such things. The elders were very adamant about resisting temptation. Bron even said Elder Bochman would be giving a speech before the ceremony about being strong and brave in the face of that temptation. Vlad grinned. Technically, he had not been given that speech, so his little slip of etiquette could be forgiven.

His bride was the most gorgeous thing he had ever seen. Clara didn't smile, but he could easily forgive her that. Surely she was tired, and nervous, and perhaps scared of being on a new planet without her friends and family. At least the brides who came from the main bridal ship traveled in a pack. Clara was alone. That easily accounted for her reserved behavior. Once she'd slept more and had a decent meal, everything would fall into place.

He reached to pull the covers over her body and paused. Two faint handprints were outlined in red on her breasts. The coloration was subtle, so much so he'd almost missed it. By the size, they were her hands. He didn't remember her gripping herself that hard. A slight smile came to him and he forced the mounting desire back into his gut. Vlad covered her with a blanket.

He saw their future clearly. First, they would explore each other and finish what had been started between them. Then they would explore the wilderness—camping, running, hiking through nature—where he could show her the things she'd only seen through a viewing screen. She had a great heart. The way she worried about feeding those less fortunate than herself proved that. He didn't think much of her society's custom of forcing orphaned children to serve in another's home, but he could hardly fault her for the laws of her home world. After the wilderness, he would take her to the village where he'd been born. There, life was simple. There were no castles, no servants, no titles, just people. His people.

Vlad loved his brothers. Just as he had loved his adoptive parents. They were good people. But there was always a part of him that felt he did not belong fully in the world of noblemen. He had a wildness in his soul, a freedom that burned so bright it needed to be released. Yes, he would do the duty his life had dealt him without complaint, but he did not feel like he was a nobleman. Lord Vladan was a title. He was born Vlad. He was just a man.

Vlad smiled at his sleeping bride as he ducked out of the makeshift room to give her quiet. Tonight he was blessed by the gods.

5

CLARA KNEW she was not in her own bed before her eyes opened. It wasn't one thing exactly, but a combination of strange sensations that caused a thread of apprehension to flow over her body to settle in her stomach. The mattress was too soft, the air was too cool and the sounds coming from outside too unfamiliar. Normally, she awoke to the feel of her handmaids touching her. They started working on her hair and feet before she fully awoke in the morning. She'd gotten used to sleeping through the attentions of their administering hands.

Clara turned to the side of the tent. Distant shouts forced her from the bed. Only when her feet hit the floor did she realize she'd slept naked. The realization brought forth the memory of the night before.

You are very sweet, bride.

Sweet. Vlad had called her sweet.

Clara sniffed her arm and flicked her tongue on her flesh. She hardly tasted sweet. He had to mean it as the endearment of the word.

She wasn't sure what to make of what had happened between them during his scrutiny of her. Perhaps she had been overtired from her journey, overwrought from her new home world, overcome from being left alone amongst half-naked primitives. No. All those things were excuses. She was a lady and she had failed to act as one the night before as she let her body get carried away by her husband's inspection. Due to the stress of her circumstance, she could forgive herself this one slip. But it would not, *could not* happen again. The last thing her mother had said to her when she left was, "Remember the lady I have raised you to be. You represent all of your family with each action you take. I mourn your going but rejoice in the next generation."

Clara lifted her hand and let it hover in the air, pretending her mother stood before her. The familiar act brought her a little comfort, false as the comfort was. Whispering into the tent, she said, "I will do what you wish, Mother. Always as you wish."

One year to get pregnant. That was manageable. The mandatory night in a tent was over. Now they would go to his noble home where she would be more in her element. If the home was not to her standard, she would make it to her standard. Perhaps she could leave it better than she found it. Regardless, anything was better than sleeping in a tent with dirt floors.

A gown had been set out for her on a low table near the bed. She didn't pick it up. Instead, she ran the back of her wrist over the material. The deep purple color reminded her of her favorite plant, razorwires. They grew in the west gardens of her family's estate outside the reading room window—deep purple vines with razor-sharp red spikes along the spines. It kept intruders from climbing up to the female suites on the fourth floor. So pretty and so deadly.

She turned her attention to her trunk. The jewel-encrusted gown was inside it—the gown of a lady, the gown of her former life.

Despite her resolve, the upcoming year stretched out before her. Her ship was gone. She was trapped on this strange planet. Having grown up in a house full of siblings, the idea of being alone suddenly terrified her. She'd been so focused on the ceremony and finding a husband as she'd been ordered to do that she hadn't thought too hard about afterwards.

Her new husband only had three brothers and four cousins. Such a small family. His family. Not hers. She had no one here.

Fear sent a shiver over her body. Her hands shook and she couldn't control them. Clara took a deep breath. This overly emotional state wouldn't do. She had to monitor herself.

VLAD WAITED for his bride to join him outside the tent. When he'd gone to fetch her she'd insisted she needed more time to ready herself. However, King Llyr and Elder Bochman didn't appear to be as patient as he. They'd come to witness the end of the ceremony. His aunt, the queen, would normally be in attendance for this part of the event, but she was busy overseeing the morning preparations at the campground below, which was why the elder stood in her place next to the king.

"What news of the others?" Vlad asked his uncle. "Did my family find wives?"

The king grinned and nodded. "Yes, nearly all. It has been a blessed year."

"Who?" Vlad asked, not needing to clarify the question.

"Mirek did not, but I am sure the gods will bless him next ceremony. We must be happy for the others," the king said.

Sadness filled him for his brother's continual bad luck.

"It is a good year," Bochman agreed. "Many blessings. The gods smile on us." The elder looked at the sky and then to Vlad. "Perhaps you should go fetch her. The other couples would surely like an opportunity to receive the king's blessing."

Vlad looked at his uncle for direction and the king nodded once. Bochman was impatient by nature and a stickler for tradition. Though he would say nothing about Clara's arrangement, Vlad knew the elder did not personally approve of the special treatment bestowed on the alien noblewoman.

Vlad obeyed, going inside the tent to retrieve his bride. He went to the flap, pushed it open an inch and said through the gap, "Clara?"

"You may enter," she answered calmly.

Vlad found her seated on the edge of the bed. She wore the enormous gown of her people. The gem-encrusted skirt was wide at the hips to give support to her elbows. Though she did not wear the wig, her hair had been pulled around the top of her head to give a miniature version of the wig's conical effect. Her face had been unnaturally paled with a white sheen of cosmetics, giving canvas to the purple on her lash and brows. The color brought out the brilliance of her eyes. She'd painted her lips and cheeks a false shade of deep red.

"I left you a gown. Did you not see it?" Vlad gestured to the trunk where the garment lay neatly folded and seemingly untouched. He knew her culture was different than his, but he'd been eager to see her dressed as a Qurilixen lady. The gown he'd given her matched the dark purple tunic he now wore. The seamstress, Arianwen, had been a friend of his mother and still lived in the village where he'd been born.

"It was not presented to me directly and, this being a proper ceremony, I thought it best to dress as a lady for the event." Clara didn't move but for the gentle rise and fall of her chest and the subtle gesture of her mouth when she spoke. Her tone was even and tranquil.

Vlad looked at the gown. It was one of the finest his people had to offer—the gown of a noble-woman. Arianwen had sewn it by hand, each stitch, and Clara acted as though it was a rag not befitted to her station.

He tried to be understanding, tried to make

excuses as to why she might be so averse to it, but in the end, the truth was her rejection of it hurt. As he looked at her, he began to question the gods' decision. How could they bind him to one of the most refined, reserved, frustratingly *perfect* creatures in the universe? Every action seemed practiced, every gesture planned. She was elegance and grace and he desperately wanted wild and passionate. He wanted her to yell if she felt like yelling. He wanted her to smile if she was happy, laugh if she was so inclined. He wanted passion not perfection.

"Are you coming out?" he asked. By the way she was seated on the bed he guessed she'd been dressed for some time. Vlad watched her face. Was she scared? Excited? Bored? He couldn't tell. "We've been waiting for you."

"I was waiting for my summons." Again, she didn't move to stand.

"They're waiting for you to come break the crystal." Vlad moved so he could help her to her feet. However, when he reached to take her arm, she lifted a fist into the air with her elbow bent. It took some hesitant gestures, but he finally realized she wanted him to hook her arm with his. Her hand did not touch him as he pulled her to standing. He felt the weight of the gown as he drew her fully to her feet. If he had his guess, he would say it weighed more than the ancient iron armor his people had used for battle in the centuries before centuries.

Clara artfully untwined her arm from his without letting her fingers touch him. The gown's skirt, by its very large nature, kept him from getting too close to her. She placed her elbows on the sides of the skirt, bent and rested on the frame. Her hands hung forward, limp. "I am ready."

Vlad wanted to ask about her composed demeanor but refrained. The two men awaited them outside and he was most eager to finish the ceremony to make her his wife. He led the way out of the tent, pausing only to hold open the tent flaps for her so she could maneuver herself under them. At her appearance, Bochman stiffened. The corner of the king's mouth twitched ever so slightly before he caught himself.

"King Llyr, Elder Bochman, may I present Lady Clara of Redding."

"Lady Clara of *the* Redding," she corrected quietly.

"Lady Clara of the Redding," Vlad repeated. She nodded once.

"Proceed," the king instructed.

Vlad slipped the glowing crystal from around his neck and presented it to Clara. Instead of taking it from him, she stepped back and lifted her arms to the side. She bowed her head, turning her eyes briefly to the ground indicating he should drop it into the dirt. He hesitated before letting it fall to the earth. He'd worn it for so long that his neck felt bare without its gentle weight.

She hardly looked at the stone. Vlad sighed in slight irritation. Why was she acting so cold and distant? He'd thought their time together in the marriage tent had gone really well. He wanted to touch her, kiss her. Only, the large skirt would hardly let him crush her against his body. The stiff frame seemed constructed of metal underneath to give it shape.

Keeping her hands held out to her sides, she stepped forward. The crystal disappeared beneath the thick material. The skirt swung as she moved her leg beneath it. Suddenly, she blinked and swayed slightly before catching herself. She took a deep breath. Then, without speaking, she stepped back to reveal the broken stone. It had shattered like clear, thin porcelain.

The elder said, as was customary, "Welcome to the family of Draig, Lady Clara of the Redding."

She nodded once, not meeting the man's direct gaze.

"Welcome, my lady," the king said. "I hope you will enjoy your new home."

Again, she nodded without looking directly at the king's face. "My family will need to be told of the ceremony's completion. They will want to know I am officially married."

"I will send a man to the communications tower to transmit the happy news to your people's ship," Elder Bochman said. The king nodded in agreement that it should be done.

Vlad smiled at the men and quickly thanked them for meeting them away from the ceremony grounds. As the two dragon-shifters disappeared down the side of the hill, he turned to Clara. "Welcome to your new home world, wife. May we have many, many fine long years here. Together."

Relief filled him. The marriage was complete. Now his life could truly begin.

CLARA WAS ASHAMED OF HERSELF. She'd been so determined to act like a lady, had even worn the gown to give herself confidence, and she'd only ended up embarrassing herself during the crystal breaking ceremony. As she'd stepped on the stone it had felt as if a spell was taken off her. She'd become lightheaded, nearly falling over. No wonder the elder had looked at her so harshly. He was a rigid man with a very stern face. The fact he'd shown displeasure on his otherwise blank expression said a great deal. She'd been unable to look him in the eye. It was a wonder Vlad still wanted her after such a faux pas.

Then his words struck her. *Many, many fine long years…together.*

Clara had no intention of spending many years on the planet, just the one her parents said was mandatory for the sake of her family honor.

She didn't trust herself to speak about it when her heart hammered in her chest as if it might escape. It was a curious reaction, one she needed to monitor privately and get under control. So, instead, she told him, "The majority of my trunks should already be on their way to your estate. I am told it is a castle. The ones inside the tent are ready for transport if you would like to call the servants. They will need to roll the material I placed on the floor to cover the ground. I hope it can be adequately cleaned. Obviously I cannot wear anything made from it now, but I'm sure some of the less fortunate families will make use of it."

Vlad arched his brow.

"I know you claim you do not have poor, but I am sure someone can use the material," she insisted.

"I have someone in mind," he answered.

"I am assuming you would like to leave for your home immediately as the ceremony is now concluded. The queen did not extend an invitation to the palace, which is understandable considering she has four sons getting married this day, so our duty here is finished. Unless I was misinformed about the steps involved?"

"No, you're right. We are married," Vlad said.

"Will we be traveling by ground or by ship to your home?" she asked.

"We'll be traveling by ceffyl." His words were slow and guarded. She relaxed a little at his steady tone.

"Ceffyl? I am unfamiliar with this type of transport but I am sure your carriage is adequate." Since she knew the names of many spaceships, she assumed a ceffyl was a type of carriage. Clara nodded once. "Since there is no escort companion to attend me at the moment, I will wait in the tent while you gather the servants and call for the ceffyl."

Vlad glanced over her gown. "You should prepare for travel."

"I am prepared, thank you. I ate a lady's portion of the fruit at dawn and will be sustained until midday. My trunks are packed. There is nothing left for me to prepare."

He gestured to encompass her clothing. "You might want to change for comfort. We're heading up over the mountain paths..."

"I am comfortable."

"Your gown is not practical for the journey. It is too heavy for the ceffyl to carry."

At that, she looked down. Her lips parted but no words came out. She nodded. There was comfort in the familiar weight of the gown, in knowing she carried a small fortune so close to her body.

"The gown I provided for you will be more suited to travel. The servants will ensure your belongings are carted to the castle where they will be safe. You can put that dress with the others you brought."

Clara didn't want to let the gown out of her sight, but she had little choice. Vlad had given her no reason not to trust him, yet she felt very isolated and alone on the foreign planet. But what could she say to such a direct command? If the transport they took could not take the extra weight, she couldn't very well protest. She nodded again. "I will do what you wish, husband."

Clara didn't meet his eyes as she turned toward the tent to do her duty. If she disobeyed, would he send her back to her family? She was married, but she was not pregnant. The idea caused a new fear to work its way inside her mind. What if he didn't get her pregnant right away? Like all her sisters, she'd been tested by the finest Redde doctors, and knew she was fertile. She needed to be pregnant. It would show her family she'd tried and her parents would then allow her to come home. It was bad enough she did not plan on having over ten children, but to have none without a medical excuse?

"My lady?" Vlad asked behind her.

Clara realized she's paused outside the tent and quickly pushed the flap aside with the back of her wrist. Her new husband didn't follow her.

6

"I MUST REFUSE."

Vlad frowned at Clara's words. His wife had changed from her gown into the one he'd given her. For the longest moment, he could barely speak as he gestured to where the stable boy held the ceffyl in place with a long rope. She looked like a true Draig noblewoman...*almost*. The gown was much more appealing to him than the steel frame of her previous one. However, she had left the bodice loose and the cross laces at the side untied. This caused the gown to hang limp down the length of her body. Only when the breeze pressed the deep purple material against her side did he detect the hint of her true curves. Her hair was still swept around her head in a cone shape and her face remained painted. None of the tresses were out of place, no wisps blowing in the breeze around her falsely pale skin. Draig women normally left their hair long and loose, like how her hair had looked the night before. The memory caused his insides to clench.

"I will not sit upon that creature." Clara stared at the large ceffyl being presented before her. A rope was tied to the horn growing from the center of its head. The skin was stretched like parched earth over a wide back. A blanket had been set on the animal, something the beast did not appear to appreciate. The creature bucked its head and the gesture shook its entire body. The stable boy held the horn down with the rope. Though hardly necessary as the animal was tame, Vlad thought the restraint might ease what he imagined would be a lady's fears.

"He will calm in a moment," Vlad assured her. As if to protest his point, the ceffyl poked out a long thin tongue, made a strange gurgling noise and stamped his hooves. "He will not hurt you."

Clara took a deep breath. "Of course he won't hurt me."

Vlad watched, confused as his wife stepped in front of the twitching beast. If the animal kicked forward it would break her in two. He started to stop her, but she seemed so confident in what she was doing.

Clara lifted her hand and held the inside of her wrist before the ceffyl's face. With one toss of the head, the creature could have impaled her on his horn. She waited for the beast to stop yanking against the rope. Reptilian eyes blinked and Vlad calmed. Quietly and with much concentration, she said, "He doesn't like the blanket." She stepped closer. "The rope is unnecessary."

"Clara, what are you doing?" Vlad asked, his voice soft. He didn't want to spook the ceffyl with his bride so close to the animal.

"Asking permission." The purple in her eyes deepened by small degrees as she looked at the back of her hand. It was a subtle change, but one his shifter eyes detected easily. If he wasn't mistaken, a ring of dark green wrapped her pupils. She turned her eyes to the boy who held the animal. "He will take us in exchange for a plant that has white petals radiating out from a light blue center, and what looks to be a fuzzy brown stem."

"A solarflower?" the stable boy asked, unsure as he looked to Vlad.

"Ah, so you have such a thing. Wonderful. Produce this plant and then we may go." Clara dropped her wrist and stepped away from the beast. "And please remove the rope and blanket. He has no intention of leaving us. He only asks for the solarflower."

The stable boy began doing what the lady asked by pulling the blanket off the animal's back.

"He told you he wanted a solarflower?" Vlad asked in a combination of disbelief and surprise.

Clara drew her brows together. It was a small movement, one that would have been easy to miss had he not been watching her. "If that is what the plant is called, then yes."

"How are you not afraid? I thought you did not go outdoors?" Vlad placed his hand on the animal's back and patted lightly. He glanced at the stable boy who was watching the couple closely. Upon meeting his gaze, the boy quickly looked away.

Clara looked up the mountain. "I will manage being in the out of doors. Nature does not frighten me. I have had my sun shots. They're good for the next two years."

"I meant the ceffyl," he clarified. Vlad knew he should stop talking in front of the boy, but he had never really had the natural decorum of timing that his adoptive brothers possessed. They had grown up being wary of servants' ears. In his child-hood, everyone heard everything and didn't care, it was loud and chaotic and he missed it terribly.

"We have animals and plants inside my home— in the menagerie, the aquarium, the animal containment, the garden spot and walled courtyards." She turned to the boy. "Please go fetch this flower."

"Lord Alek does not want the ceffyls eating solarflowers," the stable boy said as he pulled the rope from the animal's center horn. "It makes them sick if they eat anything else for several days and we have to starve the flowers out of them." Then guiltily, he looked at Vlad. "I think one of the beasts got out and ate some of the queen's flower patches. I can't be caught picking another one or I'll be blamed for the whole lot."

Vlad nodded in understanding. "Yes. Best not to pick the flowers and draw it to the attention of the queen. May they grow back before she notices."

The boy sighed in relief.

"Then we must walk. Those were the ceffyl's terms for passage." Clara nodded at the animal as if he could understand the gesture and made her way back inside the tent.

The stable boy looked questioningly at Vlad, completely confused by what had transpired. Vlad gestured him away. "Take him back to the stables. I'll fetch another in a moment."

He didn't wait to see if the boy obeyed before following his bride into the tent. The thin white walls were illuminated with daylight. Crossing to the makeshift room, he found her sitting on the edge of the bed as she had been before, waiting quietly.

"What happened?" It was all he could think to ask her.

"What do you mean?"

"The animal. If you did not want to ride you should have just said." He crossed his arms over his chest.

"It sounds as if you think I'm..." She paused. Her chest lifted slowly a couple of times, as if she tried to control her breathing. "Are you saying I'm lying? Ask the ceffyl yourself if you don't believe me. I do not see the issue. His terms were simple."

"The creature spoke to you?" Vlad didn't intend his question to sound so doubtful, but he'd been around the animals his entire life. He'd never heard of anyone actually communicating with them, at least not in such a way. If anyone could read an animal it would have been his brother Alek, and even then the man was just trained enough to see the signs and read their gestures. Alek couldn't tell what the beasts were actually thinking.

"We communicated, yes." Clara held very still, though he detected microexpressions beneath her calm. He wondered at the sheer will it would take to keep all emotions so well hidden. He couldn't do it, wouldn't even attempt to try. She continued, "I showed him we wanted passage into the mountains. He showed me he wanted solarflowers and no restraints. We came to an agreement."

Vlad closed the distance between them. She stiffened as he reached for her hand, but didn't stop him from lifting her fingers up and back. He looked at her palm and inside wrist. Tiny blue veins threaded beneath her skin. Running the pad of his thumb over the delicate flesh, he felt her tremble. Though her face stayed composed, her pulse raced.

"I am very happy to hear the wilderness does not frighten you. I admit your words last night had me worried, when you said you did not venture outside often." He wondered if she heard him. Her eyes were transfixed on where he touched her hand. "You must forgive me for the assumption. I was wrong to question the will of the gods."

CLARA COULD BARELY BREATHE. Each stroke of Vlad's finger against her palm and wrist sent strange little sensations of awareness down her arm. It came in steady waves, curling along her body to settle in her stomach. There was intimacy in that simple gesture, in the texture of skin against skin.

"You are so composed," he said.

Clara tried to thank him for the compliment, but it didn't bring the pleasure the word *sweet* had. A voice in the back of her brain warned her about maintaining that composure. It was in the middle of the morning. This was not the time for intimacy.

"Your hands are so soft, as if you never touch anything."

"I am female," she answered logically. On her world that would instantly be understood. She couldn't very well go around reading people's most intimate thoughts. If they wanted her to know something, they would tell her.

"Yes," he mused, "you are very much a female."

Vlad pulled her hand to the center of his chest and held it over his heart. The beat replaced the stroking rhythm of his fingers. With his free hand, he pulled at her hair, loosening the artfully placed clasps she had hidden to hold the style in place. Slowly, tresses fell around her shoulder. The inner voice of warning grew fainter until she couldn't hear it. Her focus narrowed until the only thing she could see was the look of her hand against his warm chest. The steady *thump-thump, thump-thump, thump-thump* of his heart caused her eyes to close in concentration.

A finger brushed her bottom lip. She sucked in a deep breath and held it. Her hand rested on his chest by its own accord and he leaned toward her. He skimmed his fingers along her scalp, holding her head. The touch on her mouth disappeared only to be replaced by the heat of his breath fanning over her cheek.

With a gasp, she opened her eyes. She started to speak but he pressed his lips next to hers, cutting off anything she might have said. His kiss was gentle, soft, dry. He slowly drew his mouth along hers, not parting his lips as he swept a trail from the corner of her mouth to her ear.

"I would inspect my bride again," he whispered. He closed his lips around the lobe of her ear, turning his caress from dry to moist.

Clara pressed her legs tightly together and swallowed nervously. A pulsing began along her sex to keep time with his heart. It was a tiny flutter of a sensation but it was there. The same pleasures that had made her lose her ladylike composure the night before came rushing back to confuse her.

As he ventured his lips back toward her mouth, he placed tiny kisses to her cheek. By the time his mouth again found hers, her lips were open and she breathed heavily. His eyes remained closed and she stared at him. The wet probe of his tongue slipped between her lips. The tactile vibrations were so overwhelming that Clara made a weak, spontaneous noise of pleasure. Vlad answered with a moan of his own.

Clara pulled away from him at the sound. He blinked, his gaze meeting hers. She realized she clutched at his tunic shirt. He held her head in his hands.

"We should monitor our—"

Her husband interrupted her words with another kiss and deeper moan.

Clara couldn't think. He pressed his hands to her back, lifting her off the bed by small degrees as he worked her dress up. She wasn't sure how, but within seconds her thighs were exposed. Vlad pulled back, artfully taking her dress with him. Her arms were forced up as he undressed her. Cool air hit her flesh, puckering her nipples. The waist wrap undergarment covered her sex. The soft material was designed to protect her skin from the metal frame of her large underskirt. Rows of small hooks ran down each hip where the frame normally fastened.

Vlad's gaze traveled over her. A strange smile came to his lips as he looked at her high boots. The Draig gown didn't require the extra support, but she'd worn them for the familiar stiff comfort against her skin.

His eyes stayed on the footwear. He hurriedly tugged his tunic over his head while using his feet to work out of his boots at the same time. He threw the shirt on the bed.

Clara tried to concentrate, knew she needed to say something proper and good. Instead, she found herself staring at his naked chest. Muscles rippled beneath the skin. Before she'd tried to keep her eyes off of him, but then the wedding had not been completed. Now she was his wife. She was expected to perform wifely duties.

"It is daylight," she said weakly, nearly incoherent as to her own protests.

"It normally is here," he answered with a small expressive laugh.

"I hadn't thought of that." Clara took a deep breath. Marital acts were normally held at night, but if there was no night…

The logic that tried to pervade was once again interrupted. He leaned forward and she had no choice but to crawl back on the bed as he came over her.

"You are very beautiful, wife," he whispered.

She hesitated before reaching up to touch him. The heat of his skin caused her nerves to jump in excitement. Mesmerized, she let her palms run along his chest muscles. Tingling erupted between her thighs.

Vlad kept his weight on his hands as he moved to kiss her neck. Her hands became trapped against him and she couldn't pull away. One of his nipples stood next to the small webbing of her fingers.

He nudged her booted legs with his knees, parting them. She didn't resist. The rush of sensations was too much for her to process. Each brush of flesh became a vivid crescendo of pleasure and uncertainty. The wrap slid up her waist to expose her hips.

Her mind couldn't make sense of what she felt. He touched her face, her neck, her sides and breasts. Each brush of body sent wave after wave of sensations over her. The material of his pants faded into flesh, yet she couldn't distinguish how it happened. She curled her toes against the hard bottoms of the boots, wishing they would disappear like his clothing. They remained laced tightly to her legs.

Sometimes, like now, when she looked at him she saw his eyes flash with gold. She wondered at the genetic abnormality of such a change. Her people's eyes shifted in color so that was not so strange, but normally it was a woman thing, and never to such a large degree. Perhaps that was how his powers revealed themselves, making her want him, making her body burn with desire and need, making her mind lose all logic. So help her, she didn't care. Power or not, real or no, it felt amazing and she didn't want it to stop.

His hips kept her legs open as he moved over her. The hard probe of his body slipped along her sex. She tensed at the intimate contact, aware of what would happen and ready for it. Correction. She thought she was ready. Vlad's arousal pressed inside her. Her entire body tensed and shook. The pleasure radiated throughout her length. Then he moved and the gratification became more intense. It concentrated between her thighs. His chest pressed into her tingling hands.

Clara didn't want it to end. She wanted to explore her feelings completely. But it was over before she had the chance to process everything.

Her entire body tensed, each muscle becoming tight. She shook violently. Vlad made a noise in the back of his throat as he stiffened above her. She blinked heavily, her eyes blurring in flashes of light and color. As suddenly as it came, the tension left her. Her limbs felt weak in the aftermath of intense pleasure. When her mind began to clear, Vlad lay next to her on the bed.

His hand rested on her thigh, near the top of her boot and he toyed with the laces. "I find your footwear fascinating."

Clara couldn't seem to catch her breath. She wasn't sure how to respond. Her mind raced to remember what she'd said, how she'd acted, if she'd yelled so loud anyone near the tent could hear her.

"We lose time," she said weakly. "If we are to walk, we should go."

"There is no hurry." Vlad's tone was suggestive.

Clara sat up, unsure what to do with the overly intimate moment. The mad rush of pleasure had subsided and, though her bones felt as if they were liquid and a strange relaxation came to her muscles, she had time to monitor herself and her behavior. There was only one conclusion. She had not acted like a lady.

"We cannot remain in this tent. It is not a proper inhabitance." Clara placed her booted feet on the ground and grabbed the Qurilixian gown. "The traditional night is over. Now it is time we acted like lord and lady, as is intended."

"I will have to go to the stables to fetch another ceffyl." Vlad moved behind her but she didn't look at him.

Clara nodded and began the long process of pulling her hair back into place on top of her head. Suddenly, Vlad was standing in front of her. He wore pants but his chest was bare. Touching her elbow, he drew her hand away from her hair.

"Leave it down." He touched her cheek, brushing his thumb over her flesh. "And this white covering is not necessary. You have a lovely face. You do not need to hide it."

Her eyes drifted to his chest, drawn to two very pronounced red imprints of her hands. She gasped and balled her hands into fists. "I apologize. I…"

Vlad glanced down and chuckled as he absently scratched at one of her handprints by his nipple. "I have no complaints, wife. Whatever it is you did was very enjoyable."

Clara had no idea what she had done, but those were her handprints on him as if burned into his chest. "You should fetch the new ceffyl." She artfully skirted around him and went toward the tent opening. Her hair felt strange against her back as it stirred in the breeze. She shouldn't go outside without a companion, but she did not wish to remain alone with him—not when he looked at her like that with those expressive eyes of his.

7

"ALEK IS NOT GOING to be happy when he discovers we gave the ceffyl solarflowers." Vlad attempted yet again to draw his bride into conversation. They'd traveled for hours. He didn't mind the silence, but he also enjoyed hearing her voice.

"His terms were clear," Clara stated. She sat on the back of the beast, her legs to the side, her ankles crossed. Despite the lumbering movements, she managed to stay stiff and upright on top of the creature. "He too wanted the solarflower as payment. He did not seek us out. Who are we to say what this creature may or may not eat?"

"At this pace we should be nearing the village in a few hours." Vlad walked briskly beside her on the wide red-gray path, liking the faster pace of exercise. The fresh air, the surrounding mountains, the

ease of nature, they filled him with hope and anticipation for the future. Mountain peaks spread out
over the distance, forming a surreal view with
jagged tops piercing the green-tinted sky. From
their vantage point on the path, he could see well
into the distance. There was so much space, so
many wonderful miles of nature and freedom. The
higher up the mountain they rode, the grayer the
earth would become until there was no red tint left.

"Village?" Clara asked. "Is that what you call
the city surrounding your castle?"

Vlad chuckled. He couldn't quit smiling. "No, it
is the place where I was born. I want you to meet
friends of my parents."

"So we will stay in their castle?"

"Their home," he corrected. The light had
brightened as they walked over the endless mountain paths. Unlike the forest by the ceremonial
grounds, the trees here were skinny with thick,
willowy tops. "Or the forest."

"A castle in the forest?" she persisted.

He stopped walking. "Not every shelter is called
a castle."

"I know what a castle is." Her ceffyl kept
moving, lumbering along the worn path. The trails
snaked off in several directions, winding into the
many distances. "I speak the star language
fluently."

"Not all our homes are castles."

"Manors then? Estates?" She nodded. "A manor will suffice. Anywhere so long as it is a noble residence will be satisfactory. I assume my belongings will be forwarded to our new location, as I do not have enough gowns with me to properly represent my station."

Vlad's smile faltered some. His wife was a contradiction. As his bride, chosen by the gods, she should be his perfect match. His perfect match would not be averse to camping in the forest or staying with commoners. However, when Clara spoke she seemed almost elitist. He again found himself wanting to make excuses for her, but it was becoming harder.

"The people we are to stay with are good people," he said, thinking of the seamstress, Arianwen, and her husband, Tomos. They had three sons, all miners like their father. Tomos had worked the mines with Vlad's parents. He'd been part of the rescue crew that found their bodies. In many ways, Vlad wished Tomos had been the one to adopt him, but instead Lord Rolant and Lady Sidone had taken him in. How could he refuse the opportunity to serve the miners? With his adoptive status came the office of High Mining Official.

Clara didn't answer.

Almost desperately, he wanted to keep her in

conversation. He wanted to connect to her beyond the physical lust he felt even now. There had to be something beneath her ladylike calm and statuesque appearance. He'd seen glimpses of her personality trying to emerge.

Nervous? Maybe she was just nervous and that is why she acted the way she did.

"What are sun shots?" he asked.

"Sun shots?" Her face changed into a look of mild surprise. It took some observation, but if he paid attention he could read her microexpressions. "They are what keep my skin from being changed by sunlight. You don't use them?"

"No need. The sun doesn't adversely affect my skin." He found his gaze on her neck, taking in the creamy flesh he found there. She did have delightfully seductive skin. His fingers twitched, remembering all too well the delicate feel of her against him. The heavy lift of his arousal pressed forward and he was glad the longer tunic of his shirt hid the reaction. Although…

Vlad glanced to the nearby forest. They were alone and it was a gorgeous day. Had anyone or anything been close by he'd have heard them.

"Is there something in the forest?" Clara asked, stiffly following his eyes.

Vlad cleared his throat. "No. I was just, ah, no."

She relaxed.

"Your skin is very beautiful," he said, again looking at her neck. He liked kissing her there, near the pulse. It had sped beneath his lips, attesting to the pleasure she felt when he touched her.

"Thank you. My handmaids apply a special cream each morning before I awake, which reminds me that I will require at least three servants—two handmaids and a companion for when I leave the noble residence."

Vlad arched a brow before he could stop himself.

"Or two," she quickly amended at the look, "if three are too many. A handmaid can act as a companion as well."

He didn't answer, unsure what to say. It didn't feel right soliciting for servants. Those who served chose that life path. No one asked them to do it.

"Or one?" Clara seemed worried by the thought of only one. "I will take care of their salary, of course. There is little shame in a noble household that is without means. It happens. It is the bloodline that matters."

Vlad changed his mind. He didn't want to hear anymore. He lifted his hand to the ceffyl's horn and tapped it a couple times. The beast moved faster, cutting off the conversation, and Vlad began to run alongside it.

Despite what she had said, Clara was very glad she didn't have to walk up the mountains. The journey was longer than she'd anticipated. For some reason, she'd thought Vlad would live closer to the palace.

To discover her noble husband had little money was disheartening. It only proved how valuable her mother's insight had been when she'd hidden jewels and space credits in her daughter's trunk and gown. Surely she could afford one servant with plenty of money left over. Commoners would be grateful for the work in a noble home.

Vlad had been running for miles, but he hardly seemed fazed by the exercise. It took nearly all of Clara's concentration and balance to remain on the ceffyl's back. When Vlad's pace slowed, the animal beneath her instantly adjusted to match. Vlad took several deep breaths as he glanced around the forest. The trail had narrowed when they'd ventured into the trees. Willowy limbs swayed over-head, creating a canopy of shade. Tiny specks of light danced on the forest floor littered with tiny plants. Bright blue birds dove from the tree limbs, attacking something she couldn't see on the ground. Each time they swooped close to her she jolted a tiny bit, startled by the blurry movement.

Suddenly, a tiny laugh sounded from behind the trees to interrupt the blue bird's soft, low shrill.

"What was that?" Clara whispered. "I heard something."

"Just now?" Vlad looked at her in surprise. "The village boys have been stalking us for nearly three miles."

"What do they want?"

"They're boys." Vlad gave a dismissive gesture.

"And…?" she prompted.

"Boys stalk things in the forest," he said. "You have several brothers. I'm sure you know how boys play."

"No. We were segregated during those times." Clara jerked as she heard another laugh. This time it was louder.

"You're getting better, but not good enough," Vlad yelled. "Now come out and greet my wife, little dragons."

A group of boys instantly converged upon them like the raining of savage, yelling monkeys. Several fell down from the trees ahead of her on the path. Others jumped into view. One rolled from behind a rock. Their eyes glowed as she'd seen Vlad's do, with varying shades of gold in their depths. Each brandished a weapon of sorts —sticks, stones tied to strings, a handful of pebbles—and screeched an ungodly loud battle cry. Clara gasped in fright. The high-pitched sound startled the ceffyl whose shifting movement made her lose her balance. Since a lady touched as little as possible with her hands, Clara hadn't been holding on. She slid off the ceffyl's back, flailing in panic before thudding painfully on the moist ground.

Instantly, all sound stopped but for the gurgling upset of the ceffyl as it pawed the forest floor. A few of the boys began to chuckle, only to think better of it when Clara didn't readily stand to face them. She slowly pushed up from the ground with her elbows. One by one, the boys lost their fighting stances.

Vlad reached down to help her. "Clara, are you injured?" He instantly hooked her arm as she'd shown him to do in the marriage tent and helped her to her feet.

Her answer was a weak noise as pain radiated down to her toes from her side. The stiff boots had kept her legs straight and jarred her hip during the fall. She felt tears burning her eyes but she forced them away. Her lip trembled slightly, but she managed to say evenly, "I am fine."

The boys had all dropped their weapons to the ground and stood frozen, wide-eyed and scared as they looked at Vlad.

"We didn't mean…" one boy tried to say.

"We thought," another added before pointing at Clara's face. "She has on war paint."

"You always play with us in the forest." The tallest boy crossed his arms, almost defensively. "And she is your wife."

The way the child said it made it seem as if that was reason enough for their actions. She waited for her husband to punish them, prepared to step in and forgive as they were only children and she would hate for them to be sentenced to death for attacking a lady.

"I know," Vlad said to them instead.

Clara looked at him stunned. Her mouth opened, the pardon already on her lips. She pulled it back, not speaking.

"You meant no harm, but let this be a lesson to be more careful in the future with ladies new to our planet." Vlad waved his hand. "Run ahead to the village. I am sure your mothers are looking to feed you soon."

The boys obeyed. A few picked up their weapons as they began a new game of chasing each other down the path.

"Sorry about that," Vlad said. "I had no idea they would mistake your," he looked at Clara's face and gave a small chuckle, "face paint as war paint."

She barely heard his words. Her hip throbbed, sending waves of pain down her leg and up her back. Trying to look balanced, she leaned all her weight on one foot to ease the pressure on her injured hip.

"We're almost there. Once we arrive I'll take you to get cleaned up. Can you ride?"

Clara nodded once and weakly said, "As you wish."

CLARA STARED at the center horn of the ceffyl, focusing on biting the tip of her tongue each time it stepped forward on its right legs. The movement swayed her onto her injured side, which in turn caused a wave of pain along her body. Vlad didn't speak as he continued onward. Though she listened, a little worried the rowdy boys would attack again, she heard nothing beyond the blue birds in the trees.

The first signs of civilization came in the form of a small home set into the trees. It was constructed of rocks stacked evenly together and trimmed with planks of wood. Even rows of plants grew in a very small, very strange square of a garden spot. One of her small attackers smiled at her from where he sat alone on a large stone, not pausing in his pointless task of smacking a large stick against the ground in steady thumps.

Clara nodded once at his attention, unsure as to why he was looking directly at her like that. The oddness of the encounter took her mind off her pain for a moment.

"What is this place called where we are going?" she asked.

"Mining Village." Vlad glanced back at her before turning his attention forward once more.

The mud on her gown had begun to dry and crumble, though the material still felt wet against her hip and ass.

"That is its name?" Clara tried to shift her weight, but it did little good. No matter how she adjusted herself, she was uncomfortable.

Vlad chuckled. "Not very creative, I know. It used to be called Mining Camp, but then the miners discovered a rich vein of ore and their families built homes to settle the area and it became Mining Village. Apparently, their wives didn't want to raise their children in tents."

"Rightly so," Clara agreed. "You're not primitives."

He gave a small laugh and said wryly, "Thanks for noticing."

More homes very much like the first stone one appeared in greater frequency in the trees. The forest opened to a long valley cut into the earth. Mining Village was nestled into the rectangular valley, opening up toward a jagged cliff surrounded by a mountain view on one side and dense trees on the other. The sound of water, faint and constant, came from beyond the cliff.

Vlad led the way down into the small village to a center main street paved with stones. The village was kept immaculately clean, built with a calculated perfection of angles. Along each side of the center road, four buildings were plotted together, then another four, then another, and so on, each cluster separated by a side street that cut through at a ninety-degree angle. The four structure pattern continued along the side streets, easily discernible from her height above the village. The houses were of rock and wood and, from what she could discern, unless they were banished from the village, it appeared as if even the poorest of the Draig people were well cared for.

As they rode closer and reached the main street, she could no longer see the entire village. People came from their homes and workplaces to view the newcomers. Clara stiffened and sat as straight as she could, despite the discomfort it caused her body and the precariousness of her balanced position on the animals' back. She forced her face to tense as she stared forward above her husband's head. At least, she tried to stare forward. Her eyes kept wandering to the side as she gazed upon the people and things around her. Had she known they would have a procession through the commoners, she would have insisted he allow her to fix herself.

Vlad was much more relaxed as he waved in greeting. Several people called him by name, not title. Such disrespect would have been severely punished on her home world. Even she had to call her father "Great Lord" when in public.

She noticed some of the young boys from the forest. They were standing with their parents, talking excitedly and pointing in her direction. A few waved like they were already well acquainted with her. She nodded at them, unsure how to respond. The openly curious expressions of the crowd combined with smiles and greetings to her husband made Clara uncomfortable—not because they were nice, but because she had no idea how to respond to such things. Until that moment, she'd not realized just how alien this world really was.

Her heart began to beat hard in her chest and her hands trembled. She glanced around, hoping to see their destination—the manor he would take her to. There were only more houses. How could she monitor herself with nowhere to retreat to?

Let it be over. Let it be over. Let it be over.

Her situation overwhelmed her. The gown she wore was too thin, too indecent. The skirt did nothing to hide her natural curves. It closely matched the ladies of the village, although hers had the addition of the dragon crest, finer embroidery and her hemlines were more ornately stitched. The Draig men wore light linen tunics with the comfortably loose drawstring pants she'd seen near the palace. A few of them were covered in fine dirt, all except their eyes, which were surrounded by two clean ovals where goggles had been.

"Vladan!"

Clara forgot herself as she turned to the excited feminine voice. The woman who called to her husband was pretty, with rich dark hair that flowed down her back in large curls and a bright, open face. Her dark eyes were expressive as she ran from the front of one of the homes toward Vlad.

"We did not expect you so soon!" the woman continued. She wrapped her arms around Vlad in a tight embrace, which her husband returned.

Clara's ceffyl stopped walking and interested himself with nearby grass growing along the center street. She barely noticed as she watched the ritualistic greeting unfold. The woman's hand lingered on Vlad's arm. Clara felt dizzy.

"Arianwen, it's great to see you," Vlad said. "How are the boys?"

"They're in the mines. One of the shafts caved in last night and they're helping to dig it out,"

Arianwen said. "No one was hurt, but it is strange. I'm sure Tomos will give you a full accounting of it later."

"I noticed the men looked particularly dirty. I thought maybe the new laser drills had broken and they were pickaxing by hand." He turned his attention to the mountain and frowned.

"No one was hurt," Arianwen repeated firmly.

Clara remained on the ceffyl, but she was ready to move on past this woman touching her husband. In fact, if the ceffyls's path took the beast right over the woman, Clara wouldn't necessarily be upset by that. She pressed her nails into her palms, digging them in to keep her emotions at bay.

Arianwen suddenly turned toward Clara, as if just now seeing her. She frowned in disapproval. Clara stiffened and lifted her jaw. Arianwen smacked the back of her hand hard against Vlad's chest. "Boy, what do you think you're doing? Did you drag this poor creature through the swamps? And the gown! You're lucky I'll be able to fix that."

"Arianwen, this is my wife, Clara," Vlad said, smiling at Clara as if nothing was amiss. Clara glanced at his chest where the woman had last made contact.

"Lady Clara, please, come inside." Arianwen gestured that Clara should dismount. "You must forgive our men for their boorish manners. They have absolutely no concept of females when they first marry." She gave Vlad a stern look and he looked properly chastised. "Come, I have many gowns you can choose from."

Never in her life had Clara been in such a position. She had absolutely no idea what she was supposed to do. Vlad looked expectantly at her. Arianwen smiled, welcoming. If her mother were here, she'd faint at the very thought of her daughter going into a common household to borrow a gown. But her mother wasn't here. In fact, neither of her parents were. They had sent her to this planet, banished her to be married to an alien man.

Clara held her arm out to Vlad and he came to help her off the ceffyl. She stood, nervous, before the woman. And then she tried something she'd never really done before. Clara looked the stranger in the eyes and smiled. The gesture felt strange on her lips and she quickly released it into a blank expression. She looked at her husband, wondering at his reaction to the gesture. His face didn't change as he hooked his elbow around hers. It would seem her effort had gone unnoticed.

"The boys will be home soon," Arianwen said. "We planned a simple meal, but as always, you are welcome in our home."

"Anything you provide, Arianwen, will be

welcome. Perhaps your cooking will induce my bride to eat more than a handful." Vlad patted Clara's arm, leading her into the modest home as he followed Arianwen inside.

"Ah." Arianwen chuckled. "You're one with dietary customs, are you?" She paused at the door, looking at Clara. "You are tiny, but I'm sure your husband will soon fix that. We brides all have some quirks when we arrive here. As per my people's warrior customs, I had no hair and lines drawn all over my face. It took me months to agree to wear so many clothes." She glanced down at her long skirt. "We assimilate. Now I love sewing. I can't even imagine following in my ancestor's Malkyrie past." Then, pointedly to Vlad, she added, "But I still throw a knife straighter than my husband."

Clara found herself intrigued by the thought of a woman warrior. She'd heard of such races but had never been allowed to meet a descendent of one.

"Not much of a talker, are you?" Arianwen waved her hand as if it were of no concern. She led the way inside.

The commoner's home was not what Clara expected. Her parents always spoke as if the non-titled were somehow dirty. Arianwen's home, though packed full of items, was very organized and clean. The miniature rooms were filled with furniture. A drawing hung on the wall. She didn't recognize the beast it depicted, but it looked fierce. Material had been tucked over the couches and left to drape along the sides, which centered on a small fireplace in the wall. The only dirt she detected was on a pair of boots near the front door. They were caked with dried mud and set aside in a bin.

"Vlad, make yourself useful. Bring in firewood for me." The woman gestured that Clara should follow her. "My lady, please, this way."

Clara watched, surprised that her husband obeyed the woman's command. When they were alone in a narrow hall, Arianwen looked over Clara's face. "I'll draw you a bath first, so you can clean up."

Clara attempted another smile, but Arianwen turned before she could form it. The woman pushed open a door. Inside, a large square had been cut into the floor. Water bubbled inside it and steam curled into a vent.

"The water renews itself," Arianwen explained. "There are natural springs around here that we tap into. The minerals keep the water clean and there are underground filters installed beneath the town. I would not recommend swallowing the water. Many do not like the taste."

Clara nodded. Her eyes traveled along the smooth walls to a counter inset into the wall. The stone looked as if it had been plucked from the ground outside and carved to fit the home.

"If you give me that gown, I can repair it for you. I imagine you are very upset by the damage." Arianwen tugged at the tie hanging at Clara's waist to loosen it more.

"Yes," Clara said. "Very much so."

"Understandable. Many women feel senti-mental about their wedding gowns."

It wasn't exactly what Clara had meant, but she did not correct the woman. It seemed rude to point out she had thought more about her embarrassing lack of propriety rather than the gown's emotional value. On her world, they put more value on the actual cost of the gown than any other attachment to it.

This isn't my world, she reminded herself. Not that she needed the reminder.

"Vlad was very anxious when he asked me to sew this for him. I'm glad you are attached to it."

Clara felt instantly bad for not complimenting the garment. "It is very well constructed. The seams appear to be very sturdy."

Arianwen paused for a few quiet seconds before nodding. "Thank you for noticing." She began tugging at the laces to help Clara disrobe.

Without thought, Clara allowed the woman to assist. She lifted her arms so Arianwen could pull the material over her head. Arianwen tossed the gown over her shoulder to carry it while freeing her hands. Loosening her boot laces took a bit longer, but once Arianwen started helping, she didn't stop. She attended her task with an admirable concentration and sense of purpose.

Clara let her remove the first boot and start on the second. "I require a handmaid to work for me at the castle. There will be retraining, of course, but I would like to honor you with a place in—"

"Ah!" Arianwen let loose a high-pitched gasp as she stopped tugging at the second boot's laces. "What did he allow to happen to…?" Her voice trailed off before she yelled in anger, "Vladan!"

Clara jolted in shock at the loud noise. She glanced down her body to where Arianwen had been looking. A large dark bruise formed down her side and hip around a swollen patch of flesh. Angry red scrapes only added to the injury. It hurt to move her leg, but she'd been managing. By propriety, Arianwen should have ignored it.

The woman took the gown with her, leaving Clara to stand naked in the room with one boot on. She crossed her arms before her chest and frowned. When Arianwen didn't immediately return, Clara pulled the remaining laces with her little fingers and managed to get the footwear off herself. With the pressure of the boot gone, her leg began to throb. She did her best to ignore it.

Glancing to the bath, she hesitantly touched the water with her toe. Instant warmth curled up her leg. Gingerly, she stepped down into the bath, easing in slowly to protect her injured hip. The process of stepping down hurt and she bit the tip of her tongue.

"...medic immediately!" Arianwen yelled from another part of the house. Clara turned to the door. She winced as she brought another foot into the bath.

"What are you yelling about?" Vlad asked. He stumbled into the entryway, as if pushed. Stopping, his eyes instantly went to his naked wife, half in the tub. A grin spread over his face. "Never mind the yelling, Ari, I'll do my duty by my wife with little badgering. Be gone, woman, leave me to it."

"You call that duty?" Arianwen demanded. She stormed into the room. Clara quickly tried to cover herself, discomfited by the quickly filling space. Her husband stared at her chest. An angry Arianwen pointed at Clara's injuries. "You call that doing your duty?"

"What?" Vladan's expression fell as he followed Arianwen's gesture. He pushed his way into the bathwater, unmindful that he was dressed. "Clara, what happened? Why didn't you say?"

Clara sunk down into the water to hide.

"Leave us, Ari. Find a hand-held medic unit," Vlad ordered.

"There's only one in the village. I'm not sure who has it. I'll ask around." Arianwen seemed more docile now, at least in the volume of her tone. She closed the door and her footsteps could be heard rushing from the home.

"Clara? Did this happen when you fell?" He knelt into the water, not bothering to remove his clothing. Vlad urged her to stand, nearly yanking her to her feet when she tried to remain in the water. "Why didn't you say?"

"You did not ask."

"I did. When you fell. You said you were fine. This is not fine." He touched the injury lightly. She jerked away from him as a reflex.

"I am a lady. I cannot complain in front of others. You did not inquire again in private so it was not my place to put my burden on you without your invitation to do so."

"Taking care of my injured wife is not a burden," he scolded. "You should have told me you needed medical attention."

"I managed without it." The more worked up everyone else became, the more she found herself withdrawing into the comfort of stoicism.

"Suffered without it seems the more correct phrasing."

"The accident was not of my doing. I did not order the boys to attack." Clara tensed, instantly wishing she could take the angry words back.

"They were playing and meant no harm." Vlad again touched her hip before drawing his fingers away. "We'll fix this with the medic unit. Next time you're injured, tell me immediately. None of this *I'm a lady* nonsense. If you're hurt, I need to know."

Clara didn't like the look on his face or the censure in his voice. Nonsense? She turned her head down. "As you wish, my lord husband. Always as you wish."

VLAD STARED in frustration at his wife. She refused to look at him and he didn't want to look at anything else. The bruise on her hip was bad. He'd been injured in battle before and knew the pain she must be in. Luckily, it didn't appear as if anything was broken. Since she was so thin, it was easy to determine her bone structure.

The water adhered his clothes to his body but he didn't care. Clara kept her eyes away and her arms crossed over her chest. She didn't move except for the slight rise and fall of her breathing. It felt like a long time before Arianwen returned to the home. The woman's steps were abnormally loud, as if giving him warning that she was coming. When she entered the bathroom, she carried an older hand-held medic. Their kind rarely needed the equipment, but he made a mental note to requisition a newer model for the village. The mining office was well equipped. There was no reason the village shouldn't be as well.

"I need that firewood," Arianwen said. "The wind hitting the waterfall is coming our way. It feels as if this is going to be a cool night. I can attend Lady Clara."

Vlad nodded and slowly got out of the water. Clara still didn't move. Her face was calm, her breath even. Any reaction he wanted to have seemed silly next to her stoicism. He nodded his thanks to Arianwen as he left the room.

"Don't track water all over my house," Arianwen warned. "You know where to find a change of clothes."

8

VLAD'S WORDS stung even hours after his saying them. Being a lady was not nonsense. It was all she had on this alien world. It is all she'd ever been trained to be. To have him dismiss it hurt worse than her injured hip. The medic unit fixed up her bruised skin quite nicely, but there was no medical setting to cure her bruised feelings.

One day. That is all she'd been there. One day.

A year had never felt so long.

She refused to join Arianwen and her family to dine, pleading fatigue. The men came back from the mines. From what she could hear, there were three of them. They were loud and boisterous and greeted Vlad like a brother. Questions were asked about her, but she didn't hear Vlad's answers.

The small room resembled the rest of the house

—tidy and cluttered. Trunks lined the wall, some stacked as tall as three high. A strange statue, humanesque in design but lacking anatomical features, stood guard in the corner. Someone had stabbed it with long, thin metal spikes. The bed in the marriage tent was bigger than the one she now sat on, though the comforter was innately stitched with tiny birds and flowers.

Arianwen had given her a gown. The blue material was soft and the stitches even, but it resembled her new home world. Nothing was familiar.

Clara felt isolated and alone. Each time a shout of laughter filtered in from the other room to break her silence the feelings only became worse. Nothing on this planet made sense. Here she was a noble-woman, married to a nobleman who did not act noble. If she hadn't been assured by the king that Vlad was titled, she would never have believed it.

Pinching the edge of the blanket, she rolled onto the bed and wrapped it around her body. If she closed her eyes, maybe it would all just go away.

VLAD GRINNED at the men who were like brothers to him. They had grown up together in this very village, playing outside the mines. Only, as the three brothers Sven, Matus, Nolan went to work in the mines with their father, Tomos, Vlad had been sent to manage them as their overlord. The brothers looked like their father, all strong dragon-shifters with dark brown eyes and even darker hair. Their broad shoulders came from honest labor and made them well suited to pushing ore carts on the mine tracks. Had Lord Rolant and Lady Sidone not intervened, this would have been his home and these men his real brothers.

"I wish you three would see the signs and go find a bride." Arianwen wiggled her finger at her sons. "It is way past your time for marriage."

"And leave you?" Sven shook his head. "Never."

"What if the bride can't cook?" Matus smiled at his mother. He was the charmer. He grabbed a piece of blue bread and took a big bite.

"I want to get married," Nolan said. "But they only let us have one bride. I want two or three. When one aggravates you, you can kick her out and invite the next one to your—"

Sven leaned over and slapped his youngest brother on the back of the head. "That is why you will never receive your sign to go."

"Don't hit your brother," Arianwen scolded, even though Sven was well into his adult years. To

Nolan, she added, "Don't disrespect our culture or the gods will never make your crystal glow. And, Matus, you're being too good, so I'll figure out what you're up to later. And you," she turned to Vlad, "wipe that smirk off your face. You only encourage them."

"Yes, my lady," Vlad said, still smiling. He turned his attention to his stew as Arianwen made her way to the kitchen. Matus jabbed him in the ribs. Vlad swatted at the man's hand, smacking it away before Arianwen caught them misbehaving.

"One of you should take your father food," Arianwen said as she came back to the table with another basket of blue bread slices. "Make sure he doesn't need more help."

"I'm going out to the mines tomorrow," Vlad said. "I want to check on supplies and see the damage from the cave-in."

Sven frowned and the mood instantly became serious. "It doesn't make sense. We had the entire area surveyed before sending the drones in. Luckily, no life was lost, but a drone is trapped behind a wall of rock. We're digging it out and setting up support beams. Initial readings say the drone acted like it found a hollow pocket in the rock and crashed forward too fast because the controls were set for aggressive digging. Sonar topography from last season's tests indicated it should be nothing but ore and stone in that section of the mountain."

"Is the equipment faulty?" Vlad asked.

"This is the first sign of it," Nolan said, doubtful. "Service records are up to date."

"Life is priority." Vlad slowly stood and nodded his thanks to Arianwen for the meal. "I'll survey it myself. We have a surplus of ore, so it won't matter if we hold off digging until we figure out what happened."

"Huh." Matus tilted his head. "Do you hear that? It sounds like the ceffyl herd is taking shelter in the forest. They rarely venture this close to the village."

"The storm must be worse than we thought," Arianwen handed a packet of food to Sven. "Better tell your father and the others to come in."

Sven obeyed, quickly leaving to do as his mother bid.

Vlad listened, picking up the sounds of the beasts. They were indeed close. Until Matus mentioned it, he hadn't been paying attention to the soft noise.

"Until the morning, friends." He grinned, thinking of his bride waiting for him. A soft glow came from the room at the end of the hall. As he pushed open the door, he didn't think about ceffyl herds and mines. His wife lay on the bed, waiting for him. Her body was curled into the blanket, rolled into a tight bundle. She didn't move as he entered.

Pulling a string on the wall, he dimmed the light that filtered in from outside until the room was cast in darkness. He saw her outline clearly in the shadows. Without thought, he pulled out of his clothes and let them drop on the floor. Every sense he had focused on her—the sound of her even breathing, the smell of soap on her skin, the shape of her hip beneath the blanket.

When he crawled onto the bed, he reached for her and slowly pulled her toward him as if unwrapping his present. She made a soft, sleepy noise. The sound caused his arousal to thicken.

Once she was on her back, he uncovered her completely and worked her skirt slowly up her legs. She didn't wear the boots so it was easy to see her thigh and hip. Gently, he touched her, thinking of the bruise. There was still a little discoloration from what he could determine in the darkness, but the medic unit had done wonders in repairing the flesh. He swept his fingers up over her hip to her side before making his way back down again.

The quiet, intimate moment pulled him in. Nothing else mattered. No thoughts swirled in his brain. This was his blessing, this woman, his wife. All of the newness between them would settle in time. He was sure of it. When he touched her skin, he just knew. This is who he was meant to be with. Forever.

Vlad inched closer, letting his legs press against hers. Her eyes slowly opened, searching in the darkness but not seeing him. She lifted her hand, not touching him as her wrist ran along his arm. He tugged at the laces on her gown and worked the material until he managed to free her completely. As he pulled the dress over her head, she became more fully awake. Her eyes cleared. He watched her expression. In the dark, it appeared less guarded. Did she not know he could see her?

She hesitated before lifting her hand to his face. She kept her fingers elongated as she let her wrist smooth over the texture of his jaw. The telltale sound of stubble to delicate flesh caught his attention. Clara made a weak noise and closed her eyes.

Vlad couldn't take it. He kissed her, firmly, surely. His hands found freedom on her flesh, roaming wherever they wanted. Fingers palmed a breast, pinched a nipple, and dove between parted thighs. The wet heat of her welcomed his fingers and he pushed one inside her. At the deep probe, she pressed her hands flat to his skin. Warmth erupted where she touched him. He'd felt the sensations before when she'd left the marks on his chest. The marks had faded, but not the memory of the pleasure they represented.

Wanting to feel their magical tingling elsewhere, he guided her hand down to his shaft and wrapped his hand over hers to help her stroke him. It was better than he'd imagined. Tingling warmth shot down his erection, electrifying his balls with pleasure. He nearly came from one caress but somehow managed to hold back.

She stroked him again. He tried, but it was too much. Vlad's hips jerked and he found release on his wife's hip after two strokes of her hands.

"Cla-ara," he grunted. His entire body tensed when she moved her palm over him a third time and he had to pull her hand away.

Breathing hard, he could barely hear past the pounding of his heart in his ears. Determined not to be the only one feeling such pleasure, he aggressively parted her thighs and opened her up to his mouth. The sweet taste of her cream greeted his lips and he licked her like a starved man. He slipped his tongue inside her before replacing it with his fingers. Sucking at her clit, he stroked her deep and long.

"Mm, that's it, Clara," he said, half words, half moans, against her sex. "Get me wet with you."

Her thighs pressed against the sides of his head. He groaned in protest and firmly pushed her legs back open. Clara gasped and dug her heels into the bed. An orgasm tremored through her body. She made a weak noise of pleasure.

Mindful of where they were, Vlad surged forward and captured her cry in his mouth, stifling it before the others heard them. She caressed his arms with her wrists. He smiled into the kiss before pulling away and taking her wrist in his hand. He drew her palm to his lips and kissed the flesh there. Her fingers flexed and she gasped.

"Your hands are very soft." He rubbed his face against her palm. "So much power in them."

"Power?" she asked, sounding confused.

"You don't feel it?" Even as he spoke, he felt the tingling snap of energy against his cheek.

"There is nothing special about my hands. They are like any lady's hands." She curled her fingers forward and tried to pull away.

"Our worlds must be very different indeed if you consider anything about yourself ordinary." He let go of her wrist, watching her expression through the darkness.

She wiggled and flexed her fingers. Her eyes didn't focus on anything in particular, though she tried to see his face. "I am what I was raised to be."

He wondered at the tone in her voice, but dismissed it as the rise of his desire demanded attention. No more words were spoken as he made love to her slowly. Every inch of her body was explored and touched, most of it even kissed. He took his time, savoring his new bride, thankful to have been blessed with her. A loneliness he'd felt for so long eased. Clara filled a void he didn't know existed within himself.

This time they came in unison, a perfect blending of breathed releases and whispering climaxes. Afterwards, Clara tried to move away from him on the bed. He didn't let her go. Instead, he pulled her close, holding her back against his chest as he curled his body around hers. He kissed her ear and nuzzled the back of her neck. Words of love filled him, but he didn't dare break the breath-taking silence that now surrounded them.

9

SOLARFLOWERS.

Clara opened her eyes, dazed as to where she was.

Solarflowers. Solarflowers. Solarflowers.

She pressed the back of her hand to her head, hoping the pressure would stop the hard pounding of that one guttural word.

"Solarflowers," she whispered, blinking hard.

She pushed off the bed. It was only by luck that her foot tangled into the gown her husband had taken off her the night before. Otherwise, she might not have realized her naked state. She pulled the dress over her body. The throbbing in her head made it hard to see, or concentrate beyond that one thought, *Solarflowers.*

Solarflowers.

Solarflowers.

Solarflowers.

Blindly, she stumbled for the bedroom door.

"Clara?" a sleepy Vlad mumbled behind her.

"Solarflowers," she stated.

"Solar…?" Vlad repeated, confused.

She ignored him. The home was empty as she made her way through the short hallway toward the front door. The word seemed to echo off the walls. How could everyone sleep through such noise? Instinct told her to escape. She hurried for the door leading outside, not watching where she stepped as she bumped into something only to continue on. Almost desperate, she threw open the door. Her bare feet skidded to a stop and she fell back against the door frame.

Solarflowers!

A herd of ceffyls surrounded the house, crowding the street down the block. At her appearance, their eyes seemed to focus in on her. She vaguely noticed people behind the herd, looking and pointing at the animals. The beasts tried to get closer and the image of the flower crowded her mind.

Solarflowers.

"Stop," she begged. "Please, stop…"

"Clara, what are…?" Vlad came up behind her. "What is this?"

Vlad blocked her retreat into the house with his body so she instantly slid along the side of the house. She trampled plants beneath her bare feet, but she couldn't care. The animals' eyes followed her and they made tiny movements as if they would follow her wherever she went.

Solarflowers.

Images bombarded her from the creatures, all of the same flower in different settings. Her mind translated the word echoing it inside her head. She tried to block them out, but they kept coming at her.

"Get them back!" a man yelled.

"Are they attacking?" a younger voice asked. "I've never seen them act like this."

Shaking, Clara realized she was trapped between the creatures and the forest that grew behind Arianwen's home. She lifted her hands, angling her palms toward the creatures and tried to respond. At first they became more frantic, crowding forward. Hooves thumped on the ground. They tried to surround her. Men yelled in the distance, but the noise of their shouts were far off as the ceffyls persistence drowned out all else.

"Clara!" Vlad yelled. She opened her eyes briefly to see her husband trying to push his way toward her.

She didn't answer. She closed her eyes and

pushed an image of the flower back at them. The rush of images slowed when they realized she understood them. She did it again and again, trying to let them know she received their message. Her head throbbed in waves of pain. There were too many voices.

"Solarflowers," she whispered. "I understand you want to tell me about solarflowers."

Solarflowers.

"Yes, solarflowers," she told them. Instantly, the images changed. She couldn't interpret them, not really. They were jumbled and random, coming from too many minds at once, but there was a desperation to what the ceffyls tried to tell her. Not knowing what to say, she projected the images back at them. This appeared to calm the animals and their intensity lessened.

"Clara!" Vlad's voice seemed closer. She felt his hand on her arm. "What's going on? What are you doing?"

Weakly, she blinked. The animal crowd started to depart, their messages delivered. She swayed on her feet, physically drained and emotionally spent. The beasts took a piece of her with them. She felt herself inside them. There were too many. She couldn't keep them all out and they had stampeded over her emotions.

Finding it hard to focus, she looked at Vlad. His

face was distorted and beastlike, surely a trick of her mind. She opened her mouth and moaned, "Solarflowers."

"SOLARFLOWERS?" Vlad repeated, confused as he caught his fainting wife. Her body went limp and he lifted her into his arms. He turned, ready to fight off the beasts, but they were dispersing down the village roads toward the forest.

"Vlad?" Arianwen stepped into her yard, eyeing the damage to her plants. They'd been trampled. "What's happening? Has there been a battle? Do they send the beasts here to protect the herd?"

"Calm, yourself, Ari. No need to shave your head and pull out your knives." Tomos appeared behind his wife and kissed her cheek lovingly. Tomos and Arianwen were around the same age Vlad's parents would have been had they lived, but they looked young enough to be his siblings. Such was the way of things on his planet. When people lived for hundreds of years, the hierarchy of age tended to mellow once a Draig reached adulthood. Tomos continued, "They would have sent for us if there was a battle this far north. One of the runners would have reported it."

Vlad had not heard the man return from the mines. He'd been more focused on his own wife the evening before. Tomos eyed Vlad, gave a small nod and then, appearing more curious than concerned, the man stepped out into the road to talk to his neighbors as the ceffyls lumbered out of the village.

"Why does Lord Alek send the ceffyls into the village?" Arianwen demanded like Vlad would automatically be privy to such information. She spun in a slow circle, looking in horror at her ruined garden. "There was hardly a storm last night. There was no natural reason for the ceffyls to come into the forest, let alone my garden."

Vlad pulled his wife closer to his chest. "I think they were here to talk to Clara." He didn't sound convinced, not even to his own ears.

"Talk to your wife?" Arianwen said, appearing doubtful. She turned her attention to the unconscious lady.

"Clara is special," he said by way of an explanation.

"All men think their wives are special or else the gods would not bless them with the woman."

Vlad hugged his wife tighter, focusing on her breathing, on the gentle pulse in her neck.

"Inside," Arianwen told him, waving Vlad toward the door. "Lay her down on the bed." As he walked past, she swatted him on the arm. "I swear, boy, you cannot keep treating your wife like she's a man. Every time I turn around she's either injured or passed out—and this is only the second day. You have to take better care of her. This one is clearly delicate."

"But I didn't do anything," he protested.

"Mmm hmm," she hummed knowingly. Vlad frowned, unsure what the woman thought she knew, because for the life of him he had no clue.

"I HATE SOLARFLOWERS," Clara mumbled as she opened her eyes. She lay on the bed in the villager's home, and for a moment she thought she might have dreamed the ceffyl incident.

Vlad burst through the door. "Clara, you're awake."

She jolted in alarm and instantly jerked away from him on the bed. The inelegant movement caused her legs to tangle in the blanket and she fell over on the mattress. Her heart pounded hard and fast at the shock of his sudden appearance.

"Ari said I had to let you sleep, but I've been waiting for you to wake—"

"You let a commoner dictate to you?" she asked, trying to right herself. It took some effort to control her panting breath. Had he been waiting outside the door?

"She is like a mother," he said defensively. His excited expression fell some.

"She is too young to be your mother," Clara answered logically. Her head ached with a residual pain but the throbbing was gone and she was grateful for it. She didn't pay much attention to what she said. "Even if she was old enough, you're a nobleman. I don't know any noblemen your age who let their mothers dictate to them, not to mention a surrogate."

Vlad glanced toward the wall and took a deep breath. When he again looked at her, his expression was more guarded. She should have been happy that he hid his emotion from her, but instead she found herself wondering what he was thinking.

"If our sons don't respect you they will answer to me."

The strength of his sentiment surprised her. "I should hope they would respect me. But I wouldn't expect them to automatically defer to my decisions once they become men."

Sons? The idea settled strangely inside her. Her wrist moved to touch her stomach briefly.

"If they do not listen to your opinions and deeply consider them, they will deal with me." His tone held a finality she did not argue with.

"As you wish, my lord."

Vlad moved toward the bed and reached for the coverlet. He tugged the material, freeing her captured foot. She hadn't noticed it was still tangled. When he touched her, a shiver worked up her leg. Her toes curled. She wanted him to run his hand up her calf, but he didn't. His hand remained on her foot and he sat next to her.

"Though, I will admit, I did not listen to my parents when I was young." His fingers skated up her leg. "I shifted and ran off into the forest when I was three. I stayed there for a week. My mother was frantic. When she found me, I was curled up in a nest of baldric, pretending to be a bird." His laugh was infectious and she tried smiling again. This time, the gesture caused his expression to brighten. "You have a lovely smile."

Clara didn't know how to answer, so instead said, "They probably worried you were taken by the Draig enemy. Noble children have value that way."

"The Var had no use for a little dragon living in the forest pretending to be a bird. I think the most danger I faced was from the baldric mother. The creatures don't normally appreciate intruders into their nest." His hand moved higher. "Besides, I had not yet come into my title. My parents were still alive."

Clara's attempt at a friendly expression faded. Suddenly, a few of his comments and expressions made sense. "You were an orphan taken in by nobility."

"I was."

A nobleman who was not born noble. That fact made sense too.

"And the things I said..." She couldn't meet his gaze. "I apologize. I did not realize. I did not—"

"It is fine, Clara."

"But I told you that it was your circumstance of birth that mattered, not—"

"I remember." He chuckled. "I am not insulted. I don't think all of our opinions will match, but we will work out our marriage. The gods would not have paired us if it was not possible."

She looked at her foot. Clara felt the heat of his hand against her flesh. The sensation made it hard to concentrate on anything else.

"As the High Mining Official it is my duty to see to the mines," he said. "There is a problem with some of the equipment."

"I understand. When do we leave?" She didn't pull away.

"You wish to come?"

"It is my place to do so unless you order me to stay here."

"I have no wish to order you about." The smile

returned to his features and she took a deep breath, realizing she'd gotten used to the look. "You surprise me, wife."

"I…" She didn't know how to answer. His hand stayed on her ankle.

She surprised *him*?

He lacked the refinement most men she knew carried. But then she'd rejected all suitors before him. There was something to his manner that she liked. Slowly, Clara lifted her hand and leaned forward. She hesitated before touching his face. Her fingers shook as she traced the dimple in his cheek.

"You are not like the men on my world," she whispered. "I don't always know how to read your expressions. There are too many changes in your face. Sometimes, inside, I feel as if you're disappointed in me, yet you smile. You laugh to yourself when there is nothing funny said. The others do it as well. Their faces and gestures do not always match what is going on inside them. I find it confusing and complicated. And none of you block yourselves from others. It makes it impossible to reason who is feeling what in a large group." Before he could respond, for she detected the urge bubbling inside of him to do so and was not sure she could handle what he might say, she quickly changed the topic, "Let me see you shifted. I sensed the ability in you in our wedding tent when you took my hand. There is a tethered beast inside you."

Vlad's answer came in the hardening of flesh beneath her hand. His eyes flecked with gold, swirling as if to call her mind into his. She countered the magnetic pull. The ceffyls had drained her earlier and she could not let him inside her. The animals should never have gotten past her emotional guard, but there had been too many of them to fight. Even now, she could pull up the strange, and somewhat morbid, images they'd given her to look at.

Vlad's skin continued to harden, turning a dark brown as it grew down his neck to disappear beneath his clothes. A line grew out from his forehead, pushed forward to make a hard plate of impermeable tissue over his nose and brow. Talons grew from his nail beds and deadly fangs grew from his mouth.

She studied him, unafraid. In this form his emotions became muted and easier to accept. "This is amazing." She tapped her palm against his cheek. "Your body is like armor." She moved her fingers down his neck. "Can you be injured?"

"Why? Do you wish to stab me?" His voice was gravelly and coarse.

She tapped him again. "I am surprised the

Federation did not recruit your people into a breeding program. They tried to on our planet, but we proved too difficult to negotiate with."

His skin slowly shifted back to firm flesh, but the light stayed in his eyes. "We do not belong to the Federation. Why search the stars when we already have perfection before us."

Though he spoke of his home world, she felt the compliment was for her by the way his gaze moved over her face.

"As to breeding programs," he continued, "we only mate with those the gods show us."

"Then you had never…" She felt heat trying to flood her face.

"Young men find pleasure with certain traveling women, for they are men and sometimes hundreds of years can pass without a bride, but this is nothing I care to discuss with my wife. None of that matters." His eyes swirled with brighter gold. "The moment I saw you, there could be no one else. You are my fate and I am a very lucky man. I will spend the rest of my life proving I deserve you."

Her lips curled up in pleasure and she couldn't control it. For the first time in her life, she didn't think to try.

Clara's smile fueled his. "I do not know what

the ceffyls wanted with you, but I do like the change. You appear more relaxed."

"They wanted to tell me about solarflowers. They seemed insistent." She focused on her hand against his face. The feel of skin caused her nerves to tingle. The sensations worked down her arm. She trembled slightly. Everything inside her focused on him. "I believe they must be addicted to the flower."

Vlad took her hand in his and pulled it from his face. He held the palm up and began tracing her fingers with his. "It is a rare and lovely gift you have."

"It's not so rare on my world. I find it curious that something so ordinary on my birth planet becomes so fascinating for you here."

"I doubt there is anything ordinary about you, wife, on your birth planet or any other." His words were a whisper. "I think you would like to speak with my brother, Alek. He is the most gifted with the beasts. He understands them better than any."

"As you wish, my lord." Clara nodded. "Then perhaps he can translate what they are trying to tell me, for I have no idea why I should need to be told about flowers and baby ceffyls being born." She gave a small tremor. "In full detail." Her free wrist strayed to her stomach. In full graphic, bloody, slimy, wet, horrific detail. The images of birth were nothing like she'd been led to believe. Luckily, she would be asleep when it was time for the baby to be removed. She was a lady after all, and civilized advancements were to be taken advantage of.

"As I wish?" he repeated thoughtfully. "What is it you wish, Clara?"

She wasn't sure how to answer. No one had ever cared to know what she wished.

"I wish to know more about your culture. Are your powers the reason you do not touch things with your hands?" he asked.

"Yes, it is the way of our people. A lady does not touch the things of others. We have to keep our hands clean. Besides, it would be too intrusive to pry into the private thoughts of others all the time by touching them."

"And when you sit? Why so stiff?"

"A lady should touch as little as possible. We do not rest our arms on furniture. We do not press our backs to chairs. We do not lean against walls or tables."

"You do not eat a full meal. You do not complain. You do not ride upon animals who do not give you permission. You rarely smile, or laugh, or show me what you are thinking without words." His eyes moved to look at her thigh where she'd been injured. "You do not complain and ask for medical attention when you clearly need it. You bear a lot in silence, don't you, my Clara?"

"Emotions are understood when they need to be. There is no reason for strangers to read them." She stretched her hand as a talon grew from his fingertip. He continued tracing her fingers lightly, one after another, repeating the pattern around her hand. The sharp digit didn't hurt her, but instead stirred a wicked desire inside her body.

"We might have been technical strangers when we married, but that is quickly changing. Can't you feel the connection?"

Clara slowly nodded. She did. "There is no reason to show emotions. To do so only complicates things, especially between married people. I never saw my parents express any kind of tenderness toward the other. They were married by arrangement, much like us, I suppose."

At that he smiled, but this time the look was different, smaller, perhaps a little sad that she had said such a thing. Yet, inside, she felt his desire for her growing. The conflicting emotions made little sense to her.

Vlad continued tracing her hand, changing the direction of his pattern. "I can never tell what you are thinking by looking at you, but I do hope to someday understand it. All I know is when you look at me and smile, I feel pleasure. And when you do not meet my eye or lowly mumble, 'as you wish', I feel sadness."

"You do not wish for things to be as you would have them?" This surprised her, and she drew her hand from his. He let her go. The talon retracted into his finger, leaving it again unshifted.

"Of course, every person wishes that things were exactly as they would have them. However, that is not life. Reality does not bend to one's will all the time. What about what you want? Perhaps what I wish is for you to do what you wish, lady wife, even if it is against my wishes."

Clara was keenly aware of their surroundings. This wasn't her home world. This was a commoner's cabin in the middle of the wilderness. There were no eyes watching and judging, just her husband—a man practically begging her to do whatever she wanted. Here people smiled when they were happy and frowned when not, and sometimes they did the opposite of what they felt. Confusion filled her. This planet went against everything she was raised to be. Part of her wanted to fall back into the emotionless comfort of Redde nobility. Her husband's eyes pleaded with her not to.

"I want to feel inside you." She lifted her hand, wrist out and closed her eyes. It wasn't the same as looking into animals. People were more complicated. They knew the art of deceit. They were messy and draining, but right now she didn't care. She projected herself outward so that she could draw him in. The first image was that of a kiss. His mouth was on hers, exploring her deeply and passionately in the woods. Dirt marred her cheek and her husband's hands. A bird trilled and the sound echoed in her mind.

Her hand touched flesh and she opened her eyes to find her mouth moving toward her husband's. She kissed him. Parting her lips against his mouth, she said, "There is so much emotion in you. It's wild, clawing at the surface as if repressed. But how can it be repressed if it shows on your face so readily?"

His mouth moved against hers. She felt him smile against her palm. Her fingers tingled.

"Now, my turn to feel inside of you." He slid his hand along her hip to her knee. She knelt on the bed and he leaned forward, slowly urging her to lie on her back.

Clara's hand fell from his cheek, but the imprint was left behind on his skin. He pulled off his tunic shirt and tossed it aside. Her palm still tingled so she touched his chest, held still for a few moments and then pulled away. Vlad took a deep breath and held it. Again her handprint was left behind. It slowly faded, but the mark on his face remained.

"Mm, I like when you touch me like that," he said, leaning over her to kiss her neck. "It's electric current going through my nerves."

"It must be our kinds," she said, touching him on the arm to leave another brief imprint. The longer she held it, the longer the mark stayed. "Something in our biologies."

"Proof that we are a perfect match. Our connection is so strong it leaves marks behind."

Clara heard a small giggle and stiffened. She blinked, looking around the room.

Vlad pulled up. "What is it?"

Not seeing anyone, she lifted her hands to her lips. The sound had come from her. "I—" The words were cut off as she gave another small laugh.

Vlad moaned and resumed his kisses on her neck. He licked hard and sucked gently. Once she started, she couldn't seem to stop herself. Another giggle escaped her. The tight rein of control inside her slipped and she let it, choosing her husband over her past. There was freedom in the decision.

Her husband moved over her, slowly peeling her clothes from her body. Naked flesh touched naked flesh as he slid his leg between her thighs, parting them. He ventured his mouth over her collar bone, down the center valley of her chest and scratched his nails lightly over her hips. He kissed her stomach before trailing his tongue from her navel to her sensitive inner thigh.

She closed her eyes tightly, gasping for breath. Her heart raced. Every touch, every sensation became pronounced. Hair tickled her thighs. Fingers probed. He swept his tongue closer to her center longing. She ran her hands over his shoulders and head, amazed by how the nerves in her hands radiated pleasure up her arms. Had she realized touching things would be so pleasurable, she would have broken that etiquette law long ago.

Vlad sucked her clit gently. Her toes curled and her legs automatically widened, opening her body up to him. She hooked her leg over his back, touching flesh with the bottom of her foot. The firm glide of skin and hard muscle caused a shiver to work its way over her. She couldn't process the overwhelming flood of sensations, yet she couldn't even consider stopping him. Nothing mattered, thoughts escaped into pure desire.

As if sensing her complete submission to her feelings, he probed his tongue forward into her body. Soon a finger followed, working inside her to give her wave after wave of intense pleasure. She made a weak noise and turned her face to the side. She bit at the pillow beneath her head, unable to capture it in her teeth. She lifted her hands over her head, finding hold on the cool stone wall as she pressed down against his fingers.

He stroked her as he came over her. His hips forced her legs wider. He slipped his finger out of her, leaving her sex empty and aching.

"No," she gasped. Her hands slapped his shoulders to try to push him down again. Her hips searched, needing the contact to continue. A self-satisfied groan sounded over her. Through the haze of eyelashes and barely parted eyelids, she saw his confident smile.

"Please."

"As you wish, my lady," he said into her neck. He pressed his hips forward.

The hard length of his arousal replaced the fingers. She made a weak noise of approval. The feel of his cock was much more satisfying than his hand had been, and he filled her completely. Her legs fell open and she let him control the pace. Thankfully, he was as eager as she, and he thrust into her with hard, precise strokes. She arched her back slightly. The change in position rewarded her with an intense undulation of ecstasy.

His movements became more frantic and wild. Her breasts bobbed. He hooked her knee with his arm, lifting her leg up, opening her more. The shift of yellow intensity filled his gaze. Though he did not shift otherwise, she felt the untamed beast inside him. All she could do was hold on as he rode her.

"There," he managed, the sound gruff. "That's it, Clara, there."

As if obeying, she climaxed. Clara inhaled a sharp breath as her entire body stiffened. She couldn't move, could barely breathe. Tremors radiated over her. Seconds later, his release joined hers. They basked in the overwhelming sensations for a long moment before he finally collapsed next to her on the bed.

"Perhaps the mines can wait until tomorrow. I don't want to leave this bed today," he whispered, closing his eyes.

Vlad adjusted his limbs, pulling her next to him. Within moments, the even rise and fall of his breathing indicated he slept. She didn't join him. Instead, she rested in his arms, trying to process everything that had happened. Touching her lips, she wondered what it looked like when she smiled. The concept still felt odd.

"Lovely," he mumbled in his sleep. "You look lovely."

10

OVER A WEEK PASSED before they were able to go to the mines. First, Vlad didn't want to leave the bed or more specifically his wife in the bed. Then a rainstorm came and kept them inside for days, pelting the village in a continuous onslaught of water. Whereas Clara was sure the men would have easily gone out in the weather, she was grateful for her husband's consideration in not making her brave the storm.

Clara was used to there being many people in one home, she just wasn't accustomed to that home being as small as a cottage. With only a few rooms, even fewer if she only counted those where she was welcome to go, there were little options for privacy. This forced her to either hide in the guest room she shared with Vlad, or join the family. The logical choice in company was Arianwen, being as she was female, yet in many ways her hostess was as tough as any man. Plus, she was surrounded by men. Tomos teased his wife endlessly and she scolded him in return, often lecturing him and ordering him about like she was a lord herself.

The sons were all tall, thick specimens, very indicative of the planet's population. Sven watched her, always curious. Sometimes his eyes lingered too long on her face, but she did not feel threatened by him. Matus spoke to her like an equal and always remembered to include her in his conversations. If she didn't understand a reference in one of his many stories, he seemed to read that on her and adjusted his tale to include more details. The man spoke quite a lot, but what he said was always interesting. Nolan was the most incorrigible of the group. His joking often ran to the inappropriate, but he delivered his humor with such levity she could hardly find it in her to correct him and remind him of his station. Perhaps the most curious was the fact that none of them seemed to think station mattered. They treated Vlad like they treated each other. They were more cautious with Clara, but she had the feeling it was only because they did not have personal history. She could well imagine in a year's time being the recipient of one of Nolan's pranks, or the highlight of Matus's stories.

Without asking, Sven spooned more food onto the plate in front of her before helping himself to the fluffy yellow substance. The amount he gave her was well above a lady's portion. She lifted her hand in protest too late.

"You'll need your strength today," he said, stopping anything she might say. "There will be some climbing involved to get to where we're going in the mines."

Clara looked at the mound in front of her and knew there was no way she would be able to eat all of it. Already her stomach was pushed to the limit. Out of everything, that fact annoyed her more than others. They kept trying to get her to eat more and commented on her weight as if it needed to be corrected. All her health scans said she was in perfect condition. She hated feeling like they were monitoring her intake.

Vlad was seated at the side opposite Sven. His arm wound around her back and he leaned closer to her. Matus was finishing his story about how Sven used to walk in his sleep and how they found him naked in a tree chirping like a bird.

"No such thing happened!" Sven protested. "I was naked, but I wasn't chirping like anything and I wasn't in a tree."

"You were asleep, so how can you be so sure?" Nolan inserted.

"I didn't see it, but you were pretty scraped up when they brought you home," Tomos added, joining in his sons' teasing.

Clara glanced at her plate and tried a little of the fluff. It was overly sweet. Vlad reached his utensil onto her plate and helped himself to the dessert. She glanced at him in surprise and he winked. Clara nodded her thanks. There was no way she would be able to stomach so much sweet food. Already the taste left her a little gaggy in the back of her throat. She took some water to wash the flavor out. No one seemed to take note of Vlad's food thievery.

"What kind of ore do you mine?" Clara asked when the teasing died down.

All eyes turned to her in surprise, even her husband.

"You don't know?" Arianwen questioned, as if such a thing was unheard of. "I thought the entire universe knew about our mines."

"*Galaxa-promethium*," Tomos answered.

Those words meant nothing to Clara.

"It's a semi-radioactive mineral with stable properties that can fuel a space ship longer and stronger for deep space travel," Matus explained.

"Captains like it for long voyages because they need less fuel weight to go farther distances."

"These mountains are loaded with it," Nolan added. "And we mine it."

Sven glanced at her now empty plate and nodded in approval. Apparently, he hadn't noticed she'd had help with the dessert.

"It's rare. We're one of the only planets that have an abundance of it," Matus continued.

"And you oversee the whole system?" Clara looked at her husband, curious. If what they said was true, it was quite possible her husband was in charge of his people's entire economic prosperity. That was a large amount of power to be entrusted to a man not born into nobility. Vlad must be very well respected indeed.

"Day-to-day operations, production, worker wellbeing…" Vlad's words trailed off as if his part in Qurilixen economics were no big deal. "The mines are a long-standing family duty. Mirek handles the ambassadorial, political side of things when it comes to shipping and trading."

"And will this malfunction injure the economy?" Clara asked.

"We're lucky there is a surplus of ore," Tomos said. "This accident won't put us behind our shipping schedule."

Vlad nodded. "We still need to find out what

happened. If the equipment malfunctioned and needs to be replaced then waiting for the parts or a replacement unit could set us back."

"Agreed." Tomos nodded. The gesture was silently mimicked by the others. Clara felt how seriously they took their jobs.

"The Federation can expedite things for you, yes?" she asked.

Arianwen stood and started gathering plates.

"The Federation has very high demands and we deal with them as little as possible. For the most part it works out to our benefit. They have little interest in us as a people, but for our mining operations." Vlad lifted her plate, stacked it on his and then handed them to Arianwen. The woman carried them to the kitchen. He continued, "As long as we mine, they're satisfied. As long as they pay for their ore like everyone else, we're satisfied."

Arianwen returned from the kitchen with a satchel. She handed it to her husband. "Send one of the boys if you're going to be late this time. I know you are always safe, but don't leave me up all night worrying because you lost track of time. Again. Here's food."

Tomos nodded and smiled lovingly at his wife as he went to her. "How is it a man can be so lucky?" He kissed her without thought of those watching.

"The gods took pity on you and sent you me," she answered, though her soft look took any seriousness out of her playful teasing.

Tomos glanced at Clara, catching her watching them. His smile turned polite before he kissed his wife once more and led the way from the home.

"Thank you for your kindness, Arianwen," Clara said as she moved to follow Vlad.

"Did you put on the rock boots I lent you?" Arianwen asked. Clara nodded. "Good. Be careful in those mines. Stay close to Vlad, he'll protect you."

The warning made her uneasy, but she nodded again as she walked outside. Clara glanced down the street, making sure the ceffyls were not still in the area. The ground had begun to dry though there were still puddles dotting the streets. She'd only just recovered most of her energy from the last mind attack. Children played in the street, shouting and waving absently as the workers made their way toward the waterfall.

There was a calmness to the men, a quiet appreciation for the morning. The path they traveled was well walked, curved down into the surrounding earth from decades of use. In a few places she was forced to hop over the muddiest patches of earth or risk ruining her borrowed rock boots. Parts of the trail were near the edge of a cliff, leading down into the thick underbrush. A few places were worn as if men slid down them on the heels of their boots into the forest below.

A breeze came by way of the waterfall, cool but not wet. The sound of water rushing on stones echoed around them. Trees grew below in the dense valley, a few of the treetops high enough to touch. She lifted her hand, letting her arm rustle its leaves. It shook, sending a red bird out of the branches with an angry squawk. Clara gasped and jumped back. The men laughed as Vlad caught her.

Vlad's touch instantly turned her attention from their surroundings to him. The fresh air became tinted with his scent. She liked the smell of him and found herself breathing deeper.

The mouth of the cave was hidden by a rock jutting up from the ground. Tomos and his sons leapt up on the rock and then disappeared down the other side, as if the movement was habitual. Vlad took her arm and led her around the outcropping to an easier entrance. Bright green vines grew along the cave's opening, spreading out over the landscape. Aside from the obvious marks of foot traffic going in, she would not have guessed this hole in the earth was anything special beyond its pretty features.

The whole of the Draig economy's fate was through this hole?

Inside, the cave opened up into a large cavern, which was illuminated by light reflecting off giant crystal formations. Smaller stones clustered the ceiling and floor, with giant columns crossing haphazardly through the large space joining floor to ceiling to walls. The columns blocked the path leading inward and the men were forced to climb over the structures.

Clara touched the crystal with the back of her wrist. The smooth, cool texture was slick. Though the men didn't seem to have a problem with climbing, Clara looked doubtfully at her skirts.

"I'll help you," Vlad said. "Follow my steps."

Clara nervously nodded. The rock boots' tread adhered to the crystal's surface, giving her traction. Vlad climbed ahead of her and reached down to take her hand. Her fingers tingled where she touched him, but she held on and let him pull her up. Standing on the crystal, she smiled proudly. For the men it might be one tiny feat, but for her she'd just climbed her first rock. Such a thing would never be allowed on her planet.

"So this is where you get your crystals," she commented, gesturing to the nearby Nolan's neck.

"No, these crystals are useless except to stand

guard over our shafts," Nolan answered. "It keeps the forest beasts from venturing in."

"And the cave creatures from venturing out," Matus added as he reached the end of the crystal formations and jumped down. Clara stepped carefully from one inclined perch to another, grateful she'd worn the borrowed boots and not her own stiff pair.

"Our crystals come from the bottom of Crystal Lake closer to the palace. When our first child is born, I will take you there to see it when I get his stone so that he may someday be as blessed as we are." Vlad turned, leading her over the crystals.

Clara hid her expression as she thought of her parents' plan for her. They expected her to return home with the child and would not allow him to wear the uncarved crystal necklace of his father's people. To them, the stone would be crude and barbaric. They would insist he instead wear formed jewels and the clothing of a proper Redde gentleman. Would taking away the crystal curse the child somehow?

She didn't want to think of it, not now.

"If you could have those babies soon, Vlad, we'd appreciate it. I think the whole reason why our mother wants us to go to the Breeding Ceremony is so that we'll give her babies to spoil and sew for," Sven said.

"She secretly dreams one of us will give her a girl," Matus added.

"She thinks girls throw knives better than boys," Nolan explained, "and she wants to pass her skills forward to the next generations."

Clara made it across to the last crystal column and watched as Vlad jumped down. She reached for his upstretched hand and let him help her back to the cave floor. The exercise flushed her skin and she tried to take calming breaths. The men did not look affected by the journey.

The blue stone of the cave walls were threaded with a silvery gray. The opening only grew as they ventured downward. Loose stones covered the floor, crunching beneath their boots. The silver veins came together, giving a high glossy sheen to areas of the cave. It reflected a warped image back to her. Clara paused seeing her unpainted face and the hair wound at the nape of her neck rather than on top of her head. In such a short time, she looked so different. She doubted her siblings would even recognize her.

"Clara?" Vlad asked quietly.

"My apologies. I was thinking that my sisters and sisters-by-marriage are probably being taken out of stasis to have their children soon." She turned sadly away from her reflection. "I will miss the births of my thirty nieces and nephews." She then straightened her shoulders and stiffened her back. "I should not be dwelling on my former home. We are here to do your duty by the miners. Please, continue. I will keep up."

The cave began to narrow as they left the silver-blue room for a smaller pathway. They walked in silence a great distance until the sound of rushing water echoed all around them. The natural pathway molded into a cylindrical mine shaft. The tool marks on the walls attested to the fact this section was manmade.

A female dragon had been carved into the stone. Her fierce, scaled skin was worn from time. Around her, smaller dragons gathered as if worshipping her.

"That is Trolla," Matus explained. "Protector of the mines. The goddess keeps us safe."

"Mining superstitions," Nolan said.

"Quiet, boy," Tomos warned. "You will respect our gods."

Nolan looked guiltily to the floor and said nothing.

Vlad took her arm as the passage widened and broke off into two directions. "We are close to the waterfall."

"You can't reach it now," Matus put forth. "The crawl tunnel leading to that area was above where we're standing. The rock slide cut it off. Luckily, it is never in use for we have no reason to go to the falls."

"The shaft is just up ahead," Tomos said. He stopped near a wall of stone. "The drone is on the other side." He lifted a hand-held unit that had been left on the floor and began pressing buttons. "It's not responding to our signal anymore."

"It was probably damaged." Sven took the unit from his father and began working his fingers over it. "I tagged its last location when I was down here. It wasn't moving so I'm sure it's still there. If we can recover it, we can see what happened.

Clara didn't feel so well. She tried to monitor her breathing as she stared at the stone wall. Support beams had been lodged against the ceiling and some of the stones had been rolled to the side of the passage.

"Perhaps I should not have agreed to let you come," Vlad said quietly.

"If my husband is in charge of the mines, I must understand that duty. It is right that I came." She shivered but hid her growing discomfort. "I will maintain."

"If the readings were right, we should be close to the hollow pocket. Until we see with our own eyes though, we won't know if the drone malfunctioned and sent wrong messages or if the sonar is off and we need to replace the unit."

"I'm guessing the sonar," Matus said. "That is the only way to explain the cave-in. The shaft would not have collapsed like this if the rock had been solid. The smaller drones do not create a large enough shaft to cause this kind of damage."

"Are sonars expensive to replace?" Clara asked Vlad in concern. He nodded once but didn't seem troubled by the cost. She couldn't help thinking of how he'd reacted when she asked for servants. Then he made it seem as if he were broke.

"Lady Clara, please stand aside. Boys, let's get mining," Tomos directed. They all shifted into dragon form and began systematically moving rocks with their hands. Tomos took lead, gruffly directing the men in the Draig language. She wasn't sure how long she watched, but she was fascinated by the strength of the men in their shifted form. Curious, she tried pushing a boulder on the floor with her hip, it didn't move. Her husband and Sven had lifted it easily moments before.

Used to standing like a statue for hours at a time, she waited patiently, only moving when she needed to get out of their way so they could work. Once, she wandered closer to the opening to study the Trolla sculpture. The goddess looked wild and dangerous, none of the things Clara was. She'd reached her hand up to hover over the stone, but received no messages from the cold rock—not that she'd expected to.

VLAD WEDGED his hands between two stones and pulled hard. Rocks began sprinkling around his feet. He sensed his wife was away from the immediate area and knew she'd be out of harm's way.

"Easy," Tomos warned gruffly in their native tongue.

"The post is holding steady," Matus said in the same language.

"Almost," Vlad answered as Nolan reached in to join him.

Several smaller rocks fell as they removed the boulder. They quickly backed away, watching the stability of the shaft. Rocks tumbled, stirring a thick layer of dust. Vlad closed his eyes and waited for the ventilation to pull the dust away so they could see. The soft hum overhead indicated the vent was working.

"What is…?" Matus rushed forward. He poked his head toward the opening they'd made to look inside. A soft light shone from within, a light that should not have been there naturally.

"Matus," Tomos warned. "Be careful."

Taking his hand-held unit, Matus didn't listen

as he crawled through the narrow opening. Seconds later, he yelled through, "I found the drone."

"Vlad?" Clara asked softly behind them. Her skin was paler than usual but her expression was blank. He lifted his hand to her to indicate she should wait. She ventured slowly toward them. He heard her footfall as he turned his attention back to Matus.

"Father, you should…" Matus's words were less gravelly, indicating he'd shifted back to his human form. The others automatically did the same.

"They found the drone," Vlad translated for his wife.

"What?" Tomos went to the opening, checked the security of the hole and then crawled through. Seconds later, he yelled, "Vlad!"

"Vlad?" Clara repeated, her tone lowering.

"I will be safe," he assured her. Vlad moved to the opening to follow Tomos. Nolan handed him a couple of lights. It was a short crawl into the hollow.

The light came from the drone, which was on and running. Matus hit the hand-held against his knee close to the drone. "The signals are blocked. The unit is reading that the drone is dead but it clearly has power."

Vlad switched on a light and handed the other to Tomos. They shone the beams around.

Strange rock columns filled the space, as if holding up the ceiling. The floor was smooth with natural steps leading to the edge of an underground stream.

"Where did this come from?" Matus asked as the light hit the water. "There should be no underground water supply in this section of the caves. It's flowing in the wrong direction." He pointed toward the far wall. "The waterfall is that way. Water should flow out, not in."

Tomos knelt beside the stream. "This has been cut. It's not natural."

Vlad observed the evenly spaced ridge marks along the river bank. They did indeed look like a cutting tool had made them. "They're fresh too. This stone is not weathered with age." He leaned toward the water and sniffed. "This smells off."

"Don't touch it. I know that smell, but…" Tomos frowned. "I can't place it."

"Nolan, bring the big light," Matus ordered.

Vlad explored with his light beam as they waited for Nolan. He listened carefully but did not hear anything besides his group in the opening. Minutes later, Nolan appeared with a light. He set it on the ground and turned it on. The beam was directed at the ceiling and it bounced off the rock overhead to illuminate the area.

The first thing Vlad noticed was the columns

were too evenly spaced and had strange carvings on them. They weren't of Draig doing.

"We're coming in," Sven said.

Vlad held up his hand toward the opening, "No, wait."

It was too late. Sven had already entered and was helping Clara through the hole. She unhooked her elbow from Sven as she stood to her feet. He noticed the darker color of her eyes as she looked at the area and wondered at her physical reaction to the place.

"Are these ruins?" she asked.

"No. These are not of Draig doing," Matus answered.

"Then...?" Clara prompted.

"We don't know," Matus said.

Vlad automatically moved closer to his wife. Perhaps he should not have allowed her to come. When she'd offered, he thought this would be a simple task and would give her a chance to see the mines.

"My lord," she whispered to him. Her hand trembled slightly. "You bid me to tell you when I had a medical issue. I do not feel well now."

He placed his hand on her shoulder to calm her nerves and placed a quick kiss on her head. "I will protect you. We shouldn't be here long."

Vlad hadn't expected to prove his words so

soon, but almost the second he said them, the low hum of an engine sounded behind the rock. The men instantly formed a half circle around Clara and faced the noise.

"The Var?" Nolan asked, specifying their ancient enemy, the cat-shifters.

"They don't come this far north," Tomos denied. "They wouldn't dare. They have no interest in our mines."

"I don't feel so…" Clara whispered behind him, her words weak.

Vlad listened to her heavy breathing as he kept his eyes on the far side of the cavern. The noise grew. He backed up toward the hollow's opening.

The water began to ripple in the stream.

"The water is changing directions," Matus noted.

"Clara, if I tell you to run, get through the opening and run," Vlad said. "Try to make it back to the village."

A strange alien craft surfaced. Its circular shape rotated around a center support to propel it forward. The support pressed to the sides of the new waterway with metal teeth cutting into the grooves they'd been examining earlier. It towed a load of raw ore behind it, the minerals wrapped in a thick sheet of molded plastic to keep it dry.

"He doesn't see us," Matus said under his breath.

The vehicle slowed as if it might stop.

"Nolan, take my wife——" Vlad ordered.

It was almost too late. The sphere transport opened.

"Clara, go," Vlad whispered frantically.

The men shifted, ready for battle. They tensed, waiting to see what great foe dared to steal from their mines. A short alien stepped out of the unit and hopped onto the ground. It landed on three stubby legs, using them like a tripod to stand. Translucent skin had a milky-white sheen to it, covering the strange pulsing blue and purple veins beneath. It was impossible to detect the alien's sex. Tiny arms stretched from the sack-like frame of its gelatinous body. It stood only as tall as their waist.

"No," Clara protested softly.

The sound of her voice drew the notice of the alien. Its face had humanoid features—two black eyes, a small nose and fat lips. A look of what could only be surprise passed over its face. Vlad dropped his guard by small degrees, waiting to see what the creature would do. The alien screeched, opening its fat mouth wide.

Tomos growled in return. Vlad took a challenging step forward. The alien began to shake, the body spreading thinner as it expanded in size. The screeching grew louder.

"Get her out of here!" Vlad yelled.

"I can't," Nolan countered. "She's…"

Vlad wanted to look but didn't dare take his eyes off the threat. Growling harshly with his shifted vocal cords, he ordered "Protect my wife!"

The alien slapped his hand forward like an elastic band, striking both Matus and Sven with one swing. Surprised by the creature's reach and strength, both men lost their footing and fell on the ground.

"What is it?" Tomos asked. Vlad didn't have an answer. He'd never seen such a being before.

"How do we kill it?" Sven yelled.

Vlad managed to ease his way to the side. He rushed forward, talons and fangs bared, and leapt, aiming for what equated the alien's chest. Punching as he landed, his hand met viscous flesh. The alien absorbed the blow. It moved with him, enveloping Vlad's fist and arm within its body. Translucent skin encased him like a tar pit while suctioning him deeper. Vlad used his loose hand to try and claw himself free. A sticky substance flowed over his fingertips. Blood? He couldn't be sure. The alien's body tried to absorb him. Strange flesh encompassed his arm then shoulder. Within seconds, he felt it sinking into his mouth to suffocate his breath.

Vlad bit down on reflex, hearing a pop as his fangs punctured the being's skin.

"Vlad!" He heard Clara scream.

Suddenly the alien screeched louder and expelled him. Vlad was sling-shotted away from the creature. He flew through the air, stopping only when he hit the rock wall. His head whipped back onto stone and he dropped to the ground in a daze. The acrid taste of fluid in his mouth caused him to gag and cough even as he tried to find his breath.

Clara screamed again, this time an incoherent sound. The alien's screech grew louder in response. Someone pulled at his arm to lift him up. Vlad tried to move toward the sound of his wife and stumbled.

"Vlad," Tomos said, sounding shocked. "Look."

Vlad stopped moving long enough to take in the situation. Clara stood with her arms raised, wrists and palms pointed at the alien. The creature squirmed in pain, writhing toward its spherical transport. It shrunk in size, almost like it tried to be smaller in an effort to protect itself. Vlad moved slowly toward his wife, awed at her ability. As her face came into view, he saw her ashen features. Her eyes were nearly green as the center ring consumed the purple. She screamed again, as if the sound was being ripped involuntarily out of her.

The alien jerked, falling back into the transport. It slapped it arms about before lifting a tiny sphere in its hand. If Vlad wasn't mistaken, he saw the creature smile seconds before it threw the sphere to the ground. The metallic-colored device shattered like glass but nothing else seemed to happen. Seconds later, it was gone.

Clara gasped and dropped her arms. Vlad caught her as she fell. Holding her on the ground, he stroked back her hair. She was damp and trembling.

"You're infested," she whispered weakly.

"Boys," Tomos yelled. "Take cover. Don't go in the water!"

The others ran and Vlad scooped up his wife to carry her after them. They dove behind columns. When he turned, he saw the drone blinking wildly. Vlad pressed Clara into the column and shielded her with his body. On instinct, he shifted and buried his head next to hers. The drone squealed seconds before a deafening explosion echoed the hollow.

CLARA COUGHED, pushing at the weight holding her down. Her arms met a chest and she struggled to see past the hair in her face. It did little good. The cavern was dark. She spit strands from her mouth as she endeavored to breathe the smoky air.

A moan sounded in the distance. Then a cough. Stones scraped stones.

"Boys?" Tomos's voice came hoarse and gruff. "My lady?"

Clara managed a high-pitched wheeze and cough for an answer.

"Father," Matus called. His voice reverberated off the hollow. "Nolan? Nolan!"

Suddenly the weight was lifted from her and she could see. Sven laid Vlad on the floor and began to examine him. "Vlad's down but alive."

The smoke began to clear as it was pulled from the room.

"The vents are working," Sven said.

"Nolan?" Matus yelled louder.

"Son?" Tomos's cry rose. "Nolan!"

"Stay with him," Sven told Clara. "I have to find my brother." She nodded weakly.

Sven disappeared into the darkness, leaving her alone with her husband. She felt along his body, over the hard shell of shifted flesh. He didn't move, didn't moan. His chest lifted only a little.

The fight had left her drained and unable to concentrate as she needed to. Her hands met the stickiness of his arms and withdrew, unsure as to what she touched. The back of her hand brushed near his waist only to bump into thick metal. She fumbled for it, blindly searching for the switch. A light shone and she pointed the beam at her husband's face.

"Over here!" Sven ordered. She directed the light toward the sound. A body lay covered in rock. "I found him."

The men worked to unbury Nolan. She placed her hand on Vlad, not taking the men's light even as she desperately wanted to see how badly her husband was injured. As long as his chest moved she knew he lived. The feel of his slow heartbeat gave her comfort. It took some of her remaining energy to feel it against her palm beneath the shield of hard flesh.

"He lives," Matus said after what seemed like an eternity of digging.

Another light turned on and Clara instantly began examining her husband. He was locked in his dragon form, unconscious. She drew the light down to his hands were she'd felt the stickiness. Bloody, charred flesh covered his hands and fore-arm. She looked at the other one. Though not as bad, it too was burned.

"I need a medic," Clara said, gingerly placing her husband's hands on his chest.

"I'll go," Sven said. The light moved with him as he crossed the distance only to stop. It shone over the caved-in wall hiding the opening. "I can't get out. Our supplies are on the other side. We're trapped."

CLARA WASN'T sure when it happened, but she had passed out from exhaustion. The last thing she recalled was being told they were trapped in the hollow. Someone must have laid her down next to Vlad and Nolan, because when she awoke she was sandwiched between the two men.

A soft glow surrounded them, flickering off

Tomos's naked back. He lifted a makeshift torch constructed of metal scrap and his clothing and stuck it in the underground river. He carried it to the torch that already burned from its place wedged between two rocks and lit it.

"The water burns?" Clara asked. On one side of them was the river. On the other was the scorched pattern centering around the metal debris of the droid. Only the columns had protected them from the full blast.

"It's tainted." Tomos glanced in her direction before eyeing Vlad and his son. He came closer and wedged the second torch into the wall. "They're chemically stripping the ore from the mines. It took me a while to remember the smell. Years ago, when I first took up an axe, these strange aliens tried to sell us chemical mining technology. I remember the event because we felt sorry for them. They looked humanoid but afflicted with strange mutations that did not appear indicative of their original race— one's face was covered in large growths, another had three extra fingers on one hand, yet another seeped white fluid from his eyes. They called their process hydraulic fracturing, or fracking. It's efficient, but its cost to the land is great. Thinking back, their mutation was probably due to chemical exposure over a long period. We're lucky the explosion today didn't set the river on fire. Trolla was looking after us. But you don't want to touch that water. We were able to start the fire from the burning debris of the droid."

Clara looked to Nolan and then her husband. They were both shifted.

"They're lucky," Tomos said. "Their dragons saved their lives and protect them even now. They'll heal faster like that, but they still need medical attention. I can't clean the wounds in here."

"What do we do?" she asked.

"We wait. Sven and Matus found a crack in the rock wall from the blast. They've gone for water and to see if they can find a way out. The main shaft is too blocked with debris." Tomos lit another torch and found a place for it before joining her on the floor near his son.

"Can we dig out like you dug in?" She wasn't sure how well she could help move boulders, but she would try.

He touched Nolan lovingly on the top of his head. "From the looks of it we'll need weeks to dig, and we don't have the supplies to last weeks."

"The others will come for us," Clara insisted. "Arianwen will come. She knows we're here."

"Eventually, yes. She'll think I forgot time again and wait a night." Tomos sighed. "When she does look, she might not realize we're inside here. It will depend on how things look on the other side after this second rock fall. Vlad ordered the digging stopped so the mines are most likely empty. No one would have heard us. They will search the open shafts and forest first. Then, when someone realizes the rocks have fallen a second time, they will start to dig."

Clara hid her fear. She appreciated his honesty, though she wasn't sure she appreciated hearing it. Swallowing nervously, she tried to breathe. The air smelled foul and burned when taken in too deeply.

"The explosion brought down more rocks. The rubble is thicker than before. I'm not sure if they'll be able to pick up our life signs from the other side." Tomos stood, leaning to get a better view of the debris. "I worry we won't have the energy to move the rocks ourselves. Our best bet is to find another way out."

Clara looked at the two injured men. Though she did not know the healing capabilities of the Draig in their dragon forms, she doubted Vlad and Nolan could last weeks without medical attention.

"Those wounds need to be cleaned," he said. "With luck, Sven and Matus will make it to the waterfall."

She nodded in agreement.

"You fought bravely. You bring much honor on your family. You could have very well saved us. For that I thank you."

"No." Clara shook her head. "Not bravely. It was instinct. The Redde do not mingle well with the Tyoe."

"You know that alien race?"

Clara nodded. "They establish profit bases all over the universe—mining, harvesting, whatever profit is to be had in a planet they try to exploit it. Most aliens let them in because they look harmless enough in their docile form, like little balls of jiggly fluid. They're also backed by the Federation who like the results they produce. They're good at what they do, highly efficient, but they will drain a planet of its resources before the hosting world knows what happened. They tried landing on Redding to harvest our trees. Our people did not mingle well. We communicate with beasts, and the psychic process, though harmless enough in most cases, boils the Tyoe from the inside out. We saw their methods when we felt into them. We can't be in the same space with each other."

"So it is truly the gods blessing that you were sent to marry Vlad," Tomos concluded. He looked down at Nolan. "I have told my sons not to question or doubt the gods. Foolish boy. He is lucky Trolla did not have him killed for doubting her earlier."

"You can't blame him for this," Clara said.

Tomos didn't respond.

"I am surprised with your ore that you have not dealt with the Tyoe before now."

"We're not Federation," Tomos said, as if that might explain it.

"Perhaps it took them longer to learn of you," Clara said.

"We are blessed you are here, my lady. From what I've seen, you can protect us." Tomos sighed heavily. "It will be a hard thing for your husband to understand. He has been raised to believe it is his duty to protect you. I know I had a hard time when I first married and discovered Ari had seen more battles than I had."

"If I stood with my family, over thirty strong, it would be easy to be rid of the infestation. The Tyoe are rarely alone. However, I am just one. If more Tyoe come for us, I won't be able to fight them. They'll drain me with sheer numbers." Clara stared at Vlad's hands. She willed them to heal. The crusted blood and charred flesh was too much and she had to close her eyes.

"But you saw their plan?" Tomos asked. "How many are there? Where are they?"

"It's not clear yet," Clara said. "I can guarantee there are more of them. You should keep an eye on the river. I should have guessed when I started feeling ill in the tunnels that they were near, but I haven't seen a Tyoe since I was a girl. I didn't recognize the signs."

"Just as I did not instantly know the smell of chemicals," he said. Strangely, the comparison gave her some comfort.

When they stopped speaking, the silence was deafening and worry started to set in, making it hard for her to breathe. She looked down at Vlad and touched his face with her wrist. Her hands were sore from the Tyoe's presence. Inside, she felt drained, worse than from the ceffyls, but she did not wish to complain. Seeing her dirty sleeve, she frowned. How had she not noticed her own state? She touched her hair. The tips felt singed on one side. Fate was indeed a strange thing. One moment she sat in the Noblae Portraite Gallery speaking to her noble father, statuesquely portraying the perfect Redde noblewoman, and the next she was trapped in a mine, dirty and singed and talking to a commoner as if he were an equal. She would bet her parents would not have predicted this fate for their daughter.

The low light shielded her dirty attire some-what, but she found she couldn't bring herself to care what she looked like. It was possible they would die in this hollow. What if the men did not make it back? What if they were trapped? What would get them first? Injuries? Lack of food and water? The smell of the chemicals coming off the river?

"How dangerous are the chemicals?" she asked, wanting to hear something besides silence. The idea of her body mutating with large head tumors left her trying not to breathe too deeply, which in turn caused the lightheadedness to become worse.

"From what I recall, large holes are drilled into the earth and then fluid is pushed into the holes to fracture the rock. The fluid is filled with chemicals that attracts the ore and helps it float upward. My guess is this river is a fracking stream. When our scientists looked at the fluid we found it to be toxic and dangerous. Without a way to make sure the chemicals are inert after use, you end up leaving active toxins in the ground or floating in these rivers to evaporate their gases into the air. The process may be faster than digging, but why would anyone want to give up the bounties of fresh food grown from the land and clean water? You cannot spray your land with harsh chemicals and not expect there to be a price to pay. No, the gods will provide as they always have."

"I suppose most people prefer food simulators and use technological water filters," Clara answered.

Tomos shook his head. He placed his hand on his son, absently checking him. "Food from the ground tastes better. Lord Mirek gave us a food simulator for the village years ago, in case there was ever a shortage. We used to dare each other to taste what was inside after too much drink. I don't think it was ever repaired after Gront struck it with a pickaxe." He shook his head. "No, we do not wish to live easy. We will live right. The easy way will lead to laziness and complacency and, in the case of these chemicals, any number of unknown medical and psychological illnesses."

For a commoner and a miner, he was well spoken. She wondered if her parents had ever spoken to a commoner. They were nothing like she had been led to believe.

"Watch over Nolan?" Tomos asked, standing. Clara nodded. "I want to listen for my sons. I don't like them being gone for so long."

Clara focused on her charges. She heard Tomos pacing for what felt like hours. He tried not to worry her further, but she felt his emotions easily enough. Time changed little of their circumstance. Time did, however, help her rebuild a little of her strength. Resting her hand over Vlad and Nolan's heads, she closed her eyes and tried to connect with them. All she found was pain lingering on the edges of unconsciousness. She jerked her hands back. Her arms ached in sympathy for Vlad and her stomach twinged for Nolan.

Clara was glad they stayed asleep. It was much better they were unaware of what their bodies suffered. Lifting Nolan's shirt, she examined his stomach.

Tomos was instantly at their side. "What is it?"

"I don't know." She revealed the dark bruise she'd found. "I think he might have broken a bone."

"Ach!"

Clara stood, eagerly watching as Matus appeared through the crack in the rock wall.

"Did you find help?" Tomos asked.

"We found the waterfall," Matus answered. He held his hand over his mouth.

"It took several wrong turns, but we found a way," Sven added. He too covered his mouth. "The air is pungent. The ventilation system must not register the chemical smell. Let's get you out of here."

Clara had been breathing the chemicals so long she hadn't noticed their potency. "I don't know that we should move them. I can stay if you need to go."

"You can't keep breathing this contaminated air," Matus denied. He went to his injured brother and lifted him into his arms. Tomos grabbed Nolan from the other side to help.

"Careful of his chest," Clara warned.

"Help me with your husband," Sven said. He picked Vlad up, carrying most of his weight. In the end, he really didn't need her assistance, but she could tell he wanted to make her feel useful.

Getting the two injured men through the crack in the rock proved difficult. It took some maneuvering, but they finally managed to pull them sideways. The stone walls hit Vlad's raw hands, making Clara flinch. Tomos handed the torches through. Once on the other side, the air, though stale, was fresher than in the hollow. The men shifted. Tomos helped Sven hook Vlad's arms over his shoulders. Tomos and Matus carried Nolan between them. Clara held the three torches.

Worry filled her as she watched her husband's dangling body. She tried to maintain calm but found it difficult when he didn't wake up. She'd had plenty of time to look at his shifted face as he slept. There was so much strength in him. He'd kept his word. She awoke with him shielding her body. He'd protected her and now paid a steep price for it.

They walked in silence, Matus and Tomos leading the way through the uneven walkways and uncut passages. The light seemed to frighten the small creatures inhabiting the cave. None of the men were concerned with the six-legged insects the size of her fist, or the tiny pale-scaled lizards the insects hunted.

12

THEY WERE TRAPPED.

Natural light shone from behind the constant wall of the thundering waterfall. At first, the fresh air and sunlight had been a blessing…until Clara discovered there was no way past the rushing water. Apparently, they would have to wait out the torrent caused by the recent rainfall. Freedom was so close and yet impossible to reach—and then the light became mocking.

This fact did not keep Tomos from attempting to climb down. He'd tried to pass through the water to the cliff's edge. The pressure of the waterfall had nearly taken him down the cliff. It was only by some small miracle that Sven and Matus had managed to pull him back inside before the man fell to his death on the rocks below. Clara felt

Tomos's pain at not being able to retrieve medical help for Nolan and Vlad. She'd never felt such depth of emotion from her own father and couldn't help but wonder if he'd brave a deadly waterfall to try to save her.

A lake of fresh water covered the majority of the cavern. Clara tended the injured men the best she could, cleaning their wounds and trying to get sips of water down their throats. When she felt inside them, she knew the depths of their pain. They needed food and they needed the kind of medical attention she was not equipped to give.

Matus, Sven and Tomos were adept at cave survival. She assumed that fact was due to their livelihood. Matus used the dry moss hanging from the cave ceiling to keep a fire burning. Tomos and Sven hunted for food. Clara tried not to think about what she was putting in her mouth, but the lizard and insect feast was hard to ignore.

"Food simulators aren't sounding too bad right now," Tomos joked tiredly at one point when he handed her a cooked lizard.

At night, Clara tried to sleep next to Vlad, but mostly she lay awake staring at his face for a sign of movement. The idea that it could take weeks for the others to come for them worried her. It was hard to track the hours by the constant light, but she estimated nearly three days passed under the waterfall's prison. She worried it would never end. Only once did she feel the sickness that indicated the presence of the Tyoe somewhere in the mines, but it was a faint nagging and one she did not share with the men. They had enough pressures trying to survive.

"Should we check the hollow?" Clara asked. "Maybe the others will be looking for us."

"It will be weeks before they can dig us out," Tomos said. "I checked it this morning. The fumes in there are strong. It might be best if they don't try to hurry their way in."

"The water in there burns. We don't dare carry a fire torch back into that place" Sven said, tapping the artificial light he carried on his waist. They didn't use it often, trying to conserve its power. "I am not sure what the air will do now that it has filled with the chemical smell. I worry what will happen if rescuers charge in with pickaxes striking metal to stone. What if the sparks create explosion? I need to get down that waterfall to warn them, to tell them where we are."

"They'll follow protocol," Matus assured him. "They will go slowly and test the air."

"Can we survive that long?" Clara stood over Vlad and Nolan and gestured to her two patients. "Can they?"

"The water is letting up." Sven said from where

he stood in the shallow lake. The water hit his thighs, wetting his clothes. "I'm going to try climbing down. I can bring a medic unit back. Something. I can communicate with the others. We can coordinate efforts."

"You will never be able to make it back up once you go down. The water is too strong." Tomos shook his head. "No, son, we must trust that all will be well."

"Matus?" Sven turned to his brother for support in his decision.

"It's too risky." Matus gave a guilty glance to his father. "The water will push you over."

"It's better than starving in here." Sven ran his hands through his hair in frustration. "If the rescuers come too fast, we could die. If they come too slow, Nolan and Vlad might not survive."

"Wait a bit longer," Tomos said. "If we are patient, Trolla will provide. The goddess is not ready for us to leave. She would not have threatened to push me over if she had been. Come, Sven, let us hunt for food. You will need your strength when it's time to go down."

Clara suspected Tomos didn't fully believe his words, but spoke to comfort his sons and give them hope.

When they were alone with the two invalids, Matus grumbled to himself, "Trolla will provide?

Like she provided for Vlad's parents? Like she provides for Nolan and Vlad now?"

"What happened to Vlad's parents?" Clara asked.

Matus frowned. "My apologies. I should not have spoken the thought out loud. I am sure your husband will be fine."

"What happened?"

"There was a thermal pocket eruption." The gravelly answer came from near her feet.

She gasped, looking down. "Matus, Vlad's awake."

Vlad's body slowly shifted to human form as he continued groggily, "My father was caught. My mother went in to save him and they both died under a rock slide."

Clara knelt beside him as relief flooded her. She'd tried very hard to monitor herself until that moment. Now she didn't care if everyone saw what she was feeling. She laid the back of her hand to his cheek. "How are you? What hurts? How can I help you?"

"Where are we?" he grumbled, blinking heavily.

Matus quickly explained their situation as Clara helped Vlad to sitting. Finishing, the man added, "Your wife has done great honor to your name. Not once did she cry out hysterically or complain. She has carried herself as well as any Draig."

"I am blessed with a fine wife." Vlad glanced at the man still on the floor. "Nolan?"

"He hasn't moved," Matus answered. She felt the man's stress hitting her like a wave and he didn't try to hide it from his expression.

Clara leaned in and kissed her husband, unable to contain her relief. He groaned at the contact. She pulled away. "My apologies, my lord, I should have waited for permission."

"Your dress is on my hand," he explained. Vlad lifted his hands to look at them and flinched. Then, keeping them up, he leaned in to her with his lips puckered slightly. "Try that again."

She gave him the kiss he sought, not letting it linger. "I am glad you are awake, my lord. I was very worried. I tried to communicate with you, but I don't think you heard me."

"I'll live," he told her. "There is no need to worry."

She felt him trying to be brave, but she knew how much pain he was in. Awake was good. Medical treatment would be better. "You should drink. Tomos and Sven are hunting. You need to eat."

"Cave spiders," Matus inserted. Vlad grimaced.

Clara moved to the water, cupped her hands

and brought the liquid to her husband to drink. She made several trips, not caring that she spilled it down the front of her bodice in her haste to tend to him. On the last run, she dripped a little water into Nolan's mouth.

"I have not done very well by you, have I?" Vlad whispered. He looked as if he wanted to touch her, but his injuries kept him from trying. "I should never have allowed you to come here."

"Then we would be dead. She defeated the Tyoe alien and sent him fleeing," Matus said. When Vlad glanced at him, he shrugged. "Small cave. Not much to do. I'm going to eavesdrop."

"Tyoe?" Vlad asked.

Clara explained what she had to the others, and then added, "I've been so preoccupied I haven't been able to sift through my thoughts properly. I know they crave the ore. They want your mines and they'll do anything to possess them. They have been studying you for some time. They know the noble Draig households. I know they have plans and I know there are more of them."

"You did not tell us this," Matus said, slightly accusing.

"It's been coming to me in pieces," she defended. "There is nothing solid to tell. I don't have their full plan and I won't until I can relax." She looked at Vlad, still very much relieved that he was looking back at her. "This is why my people don't let their emotions run so freely. We have to be reserved. It's not just a noble whim, it's a necessity. It's hard to concentrate. I'm sorry, I have been focused on you, my lord, and Nolan. I haven't pieced together more. I've been very tired trying to block all the emotions on this planet since I arrived. Then the ceffyls. I can't process—"

When her voice choked a little, he cut her off, "No, Clara, you are doing very well."

She sighed heavily, relieved to hear him say so. The conversation fell into silence. Vlad's eyelids drifted by small degrees over his eyes. She knew he was tired. Sitting next to him, she motioned that he should put his head on her lap to rest. He did, gratefully, and was almost instantly asleep.

VLAD IGNORED his pain as he flexed his fingers. His body was not healing as fast as it should. He could only guess it was from the diet of cave spiders and water. He drifted in and out of sleep, hating himself for not taking better care of his wife. Her pale features were a constant reminder of the danger she was in. His biggest responsibility in the entire world was taking care of her, and he felt as if he'd failed. When she'd been surviving, he'd been unconscious.

Matus was right. Clara did not complain—not when they handed her insects to eat, not when the only bed she had was the hard rocks, not when she cared for Nolan, bringing the fallen man water every hour even at night. Had he been asked, he would have thought his wife too delicate for survival. She'd been raised so sheltered and reserved, yet now he saw the strength in her quiet nature. If she was afraid, she didn't show it.

"Sven and I have been trying to move the stones in the hollow since that first day. Father wouldn't approve because the air in there is toxic and he worries about a spark setting the fumes on fire, but we have to get out of here." Matus kept his voice at a near whisper. They sat by the lake's edge away from the others. "We can't watch Nolan die. My father might not approve in our efforts, but we can't sit around doing nothing. The more rocks we move from our side, the faster the others will find us. In truth, we don't know how much longer it will be until they get here."

"He fears losing three sons," Vlad answered.

"No" Matus shook his head and nodded to Vlad's hands. "He fears losing four. And he knows our mother will refuse to leave the caves until we're found. With Clara in here, she has no protection from any Tyoe they may encounter. We need to find a way to warn them. Each second that passes risks much."

"The water is slowing," Sven announced from the middle of the lake. "It is time. We cannot wait. I know I can make it. I'll get help. I'll tell them of the Tyoe danger and about the fumes so they don't dig too fast and cause an explosion with their tools. We'll open the way for you and have a medic unit and supplies on standby."

"Is there a ship? Could someone fly up the waterfall and get us?" Clara asked.

"Mirek would have ships at the palace," Vlad said, "but none so small as to fly over land. They're made for space travel."

"And the way the rock face cuts back toward the bottom of the falls makes it impossible to climb back up with the supplies," Sven said. "It's a one-way trip."

Tomos walked in from the passageways carrying lizards. He looked down at Nolan. Lines of worry fanned out from his eyes.

"Nolan needs help. Clara has done what she can, but he won't last much longer on just water, and we can't get him to eat. I can reach the old rope ladder," Sven said to his father. "It should hold."

Tomos didn't speak. Matus nodded at his

brother to go. Vlad knew Sven was the strongest climber, had been since they were children. Vlad looked at his hands, hating that he felt helpless to do more. He couldn't even touch his own wife.

Clara walked to the edge of the water and watched Sven. She stood perfectly still. All around the cave was silence, save for the rushing of water between them and the outside world. Tomos moved into the lake to help his sons. Vlad pressed his forehead to Clara's shoulder as he passed and went to join the others. The cold lake water reached his upper thighs as he waded forward. It provided temporary relief to his burned hands. Droplets wet this face and chest when he neared the waterfall. Closer to the opening, the lake became shallow once more. The hard beat of water against stone drowned out any sound and made communicating with words hard. With a series of gestures and nods, Sven pressed to the stone and climbed his way along the edge. One slip and the water would take him down the cliff, pummeling his body against the rock cliff along the way.

Vlad's stomach tightened. Tomos pressed his body to the stone, reaching as far out as he could to help hold his son's weight. Matus knelt in the lake, bracing Sven's leg to give support. Suddenly, Sven's foot slipped, pushing Matus too close to the edge. Vlad dove forward, thrusting his hand between

Matus and the stone. A sharp, deep pain shot up his arm. He ignored it. His body pressed into Matus as he found his footing and together they supported Sven's leg.

"He's through," Tomos yelled, the words barely audible.

When Matus relaxed, Vlad pulled his hand to his chest and cradled it. Watery blood dripped from his arm, and he was glad for the overspray hitting his face to mingle and hide the tears of pain. Matus grabbed him by the back of his arm and ushered him toward the shore, to Clara.

"He made it," Matus said. "Barely, but he made it out. Now he just has to climb down."

"He'll make it," Vlad said, cradling his arm.

"You're bleeding," Clara stated. She looked around helplessly. "I need…" She leaned over and pulled at her skirt, ripping the edge. Then she took the strip of material and wrapped the wound with the cleanest part. "We can't keep doing this. We need to find a medical device."

"When Tomos sleeps, Matus and I are going to go to the hollow to dig our way out. Hopefully we'll reach the rescue party on the other side. If I know Ari, she's digging her way to us right now." Vlad lifted his bandaged arm. Already blood dotted the material.

"Why not send Tomos?" Clara asked. "He

comes back smelling like the hollow and if his bruised hands are any indication, he's been digging as well. You are in no condition to lift rocks."

She was right. In a perfect world, he'd let his body heal. Instead, he answered, "This is merely a test of the gods. I swore I would always protect you, Clara, and that is what I will do." He didn't wait for her to answer as he stood. Loudly, he stated, "Tomos, Matus, it's time we dug ourselves out of here."

"Perhaps we should have been digging together from the start," Tomos said. "I should have known you boys would disobey my orders to stay out of the hollow."

Vlad clenched his teeth as pain shot down his wounded arm. Lifting rocks with raw flesh while breathing toxic air was one of the hardest challenges the gods had ever given him. Thoughts of Clara kept him moving.

"Every rock helps," Matus said, as if pushing himself on. "Every one we move gets us closer to freedom."

Tomos coughed, covering his mouth.

"Go find fresh air," Vlad said, making the

words an order, not a request. "See if Clara needs help with Nolan."

Tomos nodded, coughing violently as he stumbled toward the crack.

When they were alone, Vlad said, "We are forced to go so slow that I'm not sure what we do here will make much difference. Yet what else can we do? Sit and wait?"

"Perhaps Sven should have stayed." Matus frowned. It had been two days since Sven had gone down the waterfall and they had no way of knowing if he'd survived or not. "We could have used his muscle."

"No." Vlad coughed. He tried to lift another rock, but it was too difficult. He motioned Matus to follow him as he stumbled for air. "He was right to go. In the fresh air of the other side he will be able to dig much faster than if he was with us. His muscles will be of much better use there. Plus, he needed to warn the others. It's too dangerous in here. And you know your mother. She'll not act cautiously when she is worried about her family."

Matus grabbed the artificial light and did as commanded. "I haven't wanted to say it in front of my father, but she is foolish enough to charge in here to save us, pickaxe swinging. She'll explode us all."

Vlad crawled through the crack. His hands

throbbed. Dirt clung to the worst part of his wounds. He weakly pushed to his feet, walking into the fresher part of the cave. The lingering scent of the fumes came with him, but the air was clearer. By small degrees, his head cleared.

"I cannot guess the damage that will be done to us from this adventure." Matus tried to laugh and failed. The strain of too little food, not much sleep and worry took their toll on all of them.

"If help does not arrive soon, I need you to promise you will carry Clara down the waterfall with you. Nolan and I are in no condition." Vlad looked at his hands. "If we wait too much longer you won't have the energy to hold her."

"Vlad, don't—"

"Matus, please, she is my wife. Promise me, you'll take her before you're too weak to make the trip down. Every day the water lessens a bit more. Soon it will be safe enough to take her." Vlad kept his voice low, not wanting his wife to discover his plan. She would not like it. But in this her thoughts would not matter. He would protect her, even if it meant sending her on without him. "I cannot do it, not with these hands. I can barely hold a stone."

"I promise." Matus nodded. "But it will not be today. Let us find our feast and then we dig."

"Oh, I do hope its lizards and spiders," Vlad drawled.

"Your favorite," Matus answered, just as sarcastically. They both chuckled darkly, for what else could they do.

THE FIRST PEEK of light shone into the hollow like a ray from the heavens, only to be blotted out when someone stuck their finger into it. Vlad stared at the darkness, dropping the small rock he cradled to his waist on the ground. He stumbled forward. The light came back and again disappeared.

"We're here!" Matus shouted in relief, which instantly brought sounds of excitement from the other side and a flurry of movements.

"Tomos?" Arianwen's voice came frantically from the other side. "Are you injured? Where are my boys? Lady Clara?"

"Vents," Tomos croaked.

"Tomos," Arianwen cried, the emotion evident in her voice.

Within a minute, the stench of the hollow began to lessen as someone on the other side obeyed and turned on ventilation.

"My boys?" Arianwen shouted. "Where are my boys?"

"Alive, but we need the medic," Tomos answered.

It became easier to breathe. The hole became bigger, just wide enough that Arianwen could reach through. Vlad and Matus stood behind Tomos, looking at her face and shoulder pressed against the opening. She grabbed Tomos's arm. "It's coming."

"Sven?" Tomos peered through the opening at her.

"I'm here," Sven answered.

"We almost burst through with the large drill," Arianwen said. "No one thought to check the air for gas pockets."

"She was driving it when I got here," Sven said. "Crashed into a wall when she saw me."

Arianwen's face disappeared for a moment and she could be heard scolding Sven. "Of course I was. My family was trapped…"

"Here, the medic unit." The words were muffled as a miner handed a unit through the hole.

Tomos grabbed it and then gestured to Vlad and Matus. "Go."

Vlad's body protested, but he didn't care about the physical pain as he went across the hollow to push through the crack to the other side. Matus carried the unit behind him as they rushed toward the lake.

"Clara, the rescue party broke through and…" Vlad expected his wife to be next to Nolan at her post. She wasn't.

Matus went to his brother to begin treatment.

"Clara?" Vlad called, looking around. A wisp of material on the ground caught his attention. He hurried forward, finding his wife on the ground face down at the water's edge. Her arm floated next to her hair in the water. Weakly, he flipped her over. Her drawn, pale face was scraped from a fall. Two inches over and she would have drowned. He pulled her away from the lake. Behind him, Nolan coughed. It was the first real sign of life from the man since the explosion.

Clara breathed, her chest rising and falling against his arm. He held her tight, as if letting go would cause her to slip into the water completely.

Matus appeared, pressing the medic to his arm. "For the pain." Then he attended to Clara, giving her medicine before rushing back to his brother.

Clara moaned and coughed. She stirred against him, feeling so delicate he didn't want to let go.

"It's over," he whispered. The medicine worked, easing his physical suffering. He held her tighter. "Help is coming."

13

"You saved my family."

Clara came fully awake at the sound. She automatically reached for Vlad, but he wasn't beside her. In those first seconds between sleep and wake, she was back in the mine. The softness around her confused her and she looked at the bed.

The trip back from the mines was a blur. She'd been so tired and so hungry that she vaguely remembered being carried by strangers back to the village. Somehow, she'd managed to bathe and eat a little bread and meat before falling into the dreamless black pit of deep sleep. She blinked heavily as Arianwen came into focus.

"It's the medicine wearing off," Arianwen said.

Clara began to answer but Arianwen's sudden movement caused her to stiffen in alarm. The woman wrapped her arms around her shoulders and held her tight. Clara didn't move.

"You saved my family from the alien invader. You took care of Nolan and Vlad. You went without food so the others could eat." Arianwen held her tighter. "You are the daughter I have always prayed for."

Clara wasn't sure how to react. Her own mother had never touched her like this. Slowly, she lifted her arms, arched her hands back and patted Arianwen's back with her wrists to hesitantly return the gesture. Arianwen had tears in her eyes when she finally let go.

"Until you are a mother you will never know the fear I felt when you all didn't come back. I thought…" Arianwen sniffed and shook her head as if merely thinking the thought was a sin. "It doesn't matter. My family is safe."

"Vlad? Nolan?" Clara managed, her throat dry.

Arianwen stood and went to a pitcher sitting on the nearby table. She poured a glass of water and handed it to Clara. "Vlad is tending to his hands. The burns were severe. Nolan is awake. He fractured several bones, tore ligaments and knocked his skull pretty hard. He won't be running in the forest anytime soon, but he will survive. He woke up fully this morning and is talking." She touched Clara's hair softly. "And you, daughter, what can I get for you? I will cook you anything you desire."

"Bread?" Clara asked, unsure. She held the glass with her fingertips and lifted it to take a drink.

"Bread?" Arianwen laughed, smiling widely. "You can have anything in the universe and you want bread." Nodding happily, she agreed, "Yes, you shall have the biggest loaf of bread."

When she was alone, Clara lay back on the bed. She stared at the ceiling in amazement, not sure what to think about what just happened. Arianwen had hugged her and claimed her as a daughter.

CLARA MOANED SOFTLY as warm hands touched her face. She knew before she looked that Vlad was near. She smelled him, felt him. Blinking slowly, she opened her eyes. He lay next to her. His damp hair was pushed back from his features, attesting to a recent bath. She suppressed a yawn. "How long was I asleep?"

"Nearly a full day," he answered. Warm breath fanned her neck, causing her to shiver.

"Arianwen hugged me," Clara told him.

Vlad chuckled. "I'm sure she did. She also has been spreading the valor of your deeds to the entire village."

Clara furrowed her brow. "Why would she spread news of the misfortune?"

"Misfortune? Sweet wife, you acted selflessly and honorably. You would make any man proud." He kissed her cheek an inch away from her mouth. "You are the warrior woman who took out the alien thieves."

She automatically turned her lips closer to his. "There was only one alien."

"You're a legend," he insisted.

"I didn't do anything, my lord. I simply am not compatible with that alien race." Clara tried to logic the situation. "If I try to read them, their insides boil. It's a genetic anomaly."

"A gift from the gods to protect us," he said.

"No, Vlad, seriously. I didn't do anything. Not really." Clara's voice was soft. His lips were whispering close to hers when he spoke. Tiny shivers of pleasure worked their way through her.

"A truly modest heroine, downplaying your victory." Vlad kissed her mouth, letting his tongue slide between her lips. She breathed in the scent of him. Relief filled her that it was over and he was alive. He moved his hands over her hip.

"Can you feel me?" she asked. "Your hands, are they...?"

"Hmm." He pulled back thoughtfully. "That is a good question." He tugged on the skirt of her nightdress to reveal a naked thigh. He touched the backs of his fingers along the inside of her leg and glided upward. "Yes, I think I'm beginning to feel…" He poked a finger up at her sex, slipping into the folds. A low groan sounded in the back of his throat. "Ah, yes, I'm definitely starting to detect something." He thrust the long digit deeper. He closed his eyes, inhaling. "Mmm, yes, I think the feeling is coming back now." He flicked his tongue against her lips. "How about you, wife?" Vlad moved his finger out and thrust two back in. "Do you feel that?"

Clara tensed as the wave of pleasure assaulted her. He did it again, rubbing her pussy. She made a weak noise.

He stopped stroking and she moaned in protest. Vlad pulled at the covers, revealing he was already naked. Taking her hand, he drew it to his cock and pressed it firmly against the shaft. He shivered violently. "By all the stars, your touch is like electricity."

Clara opened her thighs wider, wanting his hand back. Instead, he came over her. Her hand followed him. An involuntary jerk of pleasure hampered his movements. His mouth claimed hers even as his legs pushed open her thighs. He jerked again, his stomach tensing. She let go of his shaft and he relaxed by small degrees. Liking the connection, she pressed her hands to his chest to feel inside him. Almost desperately, he plunged into her, filling her completely. Vlad wildly thrust. He lifted up on his arms for leverage.

Clara liked the strength in her husband. He didn't shift, but his eyes glittered with golden promise. The hard pounding drew her climax from deep within. She came, helpless against the waves of pleasure as they overtook her entire body. Vlad answered her soft cry with one of his own. He tensed, releasing himself inside her.

CLARA'S EYES SHOT OPEN. "Not again!"

She hopped out of bed, not thinking to change out of her sleeping gown. Rushing toward the door, she hurried through the house. Her feet slid and she bumped into a wall as she overshot the front door. Fumbling to push it open, she then held up her hands and yelled, "I know, I know, solarflowers!"

Three ceffyls stood in the street looking at her. She quickly stepped down the path toward them, anxious to stop them before their number multiplied. Closing her eyes, she projected the picture of the flower at them.

"I know, I know. You want solarflowers," she whispered, trying to keep her voice soothing.

The creatures tapped their feet. She held her ground. They began showing her images of live births. This time, since there were less of them, she could sift through the information more easily. She saw hands, human hands, catching the babies that didn't move. The man's face wasn't known to her, but she let them know she saw. They again showed her the flowers.

Clara sighed with relief when the images stopped. The ceffyls hissed their long tongues, their attention wavering as they ignored her for the long grass growing by the gate. She took a deep breath. The sound of giggles drew her attention sharply to the side. A group of boys, some of whom she recognized from the forest, stared at her. Their grins only widened at her attention and they laughed harder. Clara glanced down to see she was barefoot and in her night clothes. Gasping, she ran toward the house.

Clara almost ran into Vlad's chest on her way through the door.

"What did they want?" he asked sleepily.

"Solarflowers," she answered. "Always solarflowers. I think it helps them cope with death or something"

Vlad shut the door behind her. "I need to go back into the mines."

Clara stiffened. "No." The word slipped out before she could stop it.

"I will be fine," he reassured her. "We'll go in a large group and take every precaution. We need to make sure the air is vented and samples are taken from the hollow. My brothers should have returned home with their brides. We'll go to our castle to meet with them. I'll have the samples tested. We'll report the Tyoe infestation and figure out a way to defeat them with the help of my brothers." He paused, kissing her nose. "And you, sweet wife, can talk to Alek about the solarflowers. Perhaps you can find a way to stop the ceffyls from following you."

Clara looked around the villager's home. The idea of noble households and castles seemed so strange to her now. She'd found more support and happiness in this little cottage than she ever had in her parent's home. Yes, being locked in the mines had been terrifying and was not something she wanted to relive—ever—but Arianwen hugged her, Tomos patted her arm, the brothers treated her like family. And Vlad, he was the most gentle and loving of men she had ever met.

"It is early. Let's go back to bed." When he smiled at her, she suspected it wasn't sleep he had in mind. Vlad hooked her arm with his and led her toward the hall to the guest room. She stopped, pulling back. He looked at her questioningly.

"I love you," she said. "I know I'm not the best at expressing emotions, but I love you. I'm glad we married. And I would like to stay on your planet."

Vlad grinned. He tugged her so she fell into his chest. "I am truly blessed by the gods. I love you, my sweet Clara. And where else would you go? This is your home."

She lifted up to kiss him, not caring that she stood in the middle of a commoner's home where any of the family could come in and see them. She knew he didn't understand her meaning, not fully, but she felt no reason to tell him her parents' plan to have her leave after a year. It wasn't going to happen. Clara would find a way to change their minds before they sent for her. She would not take Vlad's children from him. She would not leave. Nothing mattered but the feel of her husband's arms wrapping around her and the taste of his kiss. Vlad scooped her into his arms, not breaking the contact of their mouths and carried her into the guest room where they slowly made love until duty called them from the bed.

14

CLARA WAS GRANTED a ride by one of the ceffyls from the village herd after she explained she was going to tell the man from their projections about the solarflowers. This fact really seemed to excite the creatures, as evidenced by the herd following them from the village to her new castle home.

Clara glanced behind her and sighed. Yes. Still there.

The air warmed the farther away they rode from Mining Village. For the most part, the path was clear, cut through a valley of tall grass. This fact pleased the ceffyls who ate while they walked.

"If we get a land transport we would be able to get to the village quickly to visit them," Clara said.

"I am pleased you like them, for they are very fond of you." Vlad smiled. He walked beside her and rested his hand on her thigh. She looked down at the discolored skin. It was still healing and she wondered if it would always be paler than the rest of him.

"Arianwen embraced me and called me a warrior daughter," she admitted.

Vlad laughed. She loved the sound of that laugh. "A high compliment indeed."

"Do you think I'm a warrior?" she asked.

"I think you are perfection," he answered diplomatically. She liked his description much better.

"I want to give Arianwen the material bolts I brought with me if you haven't done anything with them already. If you have given them to someone else, don't take the bestowment back."

"It should have been cleaned and delivered with the rest of your belongings to our home." Vlad smiled at her. "I think Ari would like the gift very much."

They neared a forest and moved to go around its edge. A tall cliff appeared and it took her a long moment to realize it was the front entrance to the castle. Its carved stone features hid the home against the side of the mountain. It was surrounded by steep mountains, narrow passes and rocky crags dotted with lush plant life.

"My lord, why have you brought ceffyls?" A man ran out of a large rectangular structure. The concern on his gruff face gave him a harsh countenance. "Has something happened?"

"The herd has taken a liking to my wife," Vlad said. He reached to help her down. The beast she rode didn't move but tried to hiss its long tongue at her wrist. She absently pulled away to keep from getting licked.

Cenek examined her mount, feeling along its body. "These are from south of the village. They followed you all the way here?"

"My wife, Lady Clara," Vlad introduced. "Cenek, ceffyl trainer."

"Many blessings, my lady," Cenek said, acknowledging her. "Welcome home."

The ceffyl again tried to lick her. Cenek shook his head in amazement. "I have never seen the like in all my years."

"Greetings, Cenek," Clara said. "The beast would like you to give it solarflowers."

"I bet she would," he said, looking as if he had no intention of fulfilling the request.

Loud ceffyl bleats resounded from the building Cenek had come from.

"Problem in the stables?" Vlad asked.

Cenek frowned. "There shouldn't be."

"You mean there are more in there?" Clara asked. She hooked her husband's arm and urged him to escort her inside quickly. "Honor to meet you, Cenek."

Vlad chuckled as she led him toward the castle entrance.

"You laugh, but I have only now gotten one herd under control," she scolded him under her breath. Clara heard the beasts trying to follow her and Cenek doing his best to ensure they didn't charge the castle.

Through the entryway, a series of iron gates were retracted into the stone walls to give free entrance to any who might wander in. Vlad glanced behind at the herd and pulled one of the gates closed. "A precaution." Though his tone suggested that the idea of ceffyls roaming the halls looking for her amused him greatly.

A soft row of light illuminated the carved hall. The rough texture of the outside gave way to the smooth perfection of angles inside. Had she not walked into the mountain herself, she would have thought it as fine as any manor on her planet— minus the ornate details of course. The front hall split into five directions. Each route looked the same as the next.

"Our home is this way," Vlad said, pointing to the hall on the far left.

"What is that way?" she asked, gesturing over the other halls.

"Each hall is for a brother and his wife with the center hall leading to the common rooms where we take our meals, entertain guests, socialize, peruse the scrolls or conduct business meetings. The center hall also leads upstairs. As oldest, Bron will move with his wife to the tower rooms, though none of us have gone up there since my adoptive parents died." He led the way into his hall. "I will show you our home before we greet the others. Try to stay out of the side tunnels. They are a maze designed to trap intruders. After you are given access to the main computer, if you are not able to open a door then turn around, you're going into a maze."

"I will have complete access to the home?" Clara asked in surprise. "Everywhere?"

"Of course, you are my wife. I trust you, so will my brothers."

She smiled and then stopped, pointing back the way they came. Excited, she asked, "Wait. So that means they all will live with us? In this same castle? And have their children here? And your adoptive parents lived here? So I can assume when they grow all of our children will live here as well?"

"Most likely," he said, urging her to follow by walking once more.

Clara nearly jumped in a show of unladylike enthusiasm. The one thing she'd missed about her home was being surrounded by family, but it looked as if she would get that here. How could she have even thought about leaving Vlad after a year? She wanted a full lifetime with him, more if his gods would allow it. "That's wonderful news, my lord. I was so worried we'd live as a small family forever. If each wife has at least twenty children, we could populate a home of this size quite nicely and quite honorably."

Vlad skidded to a stop. Clara ignored his sputtering noises while she kept walking through the hall as it curved even farther to the left, eager to see her home. Reaching an ornate door, she looked for a way inside. There was no handle.

Vlad joined her. He ran his hand over the frame and said, "Open." The door obeyed.

"This is beautiful," Clara proclaimed, touching the door frame with the tips of her fingers. "You cannot even see the technology inside."

"Perhaps you would like to look inside the home, my lady?" Vlad asked. He didn't give her time to respond as he swept her up into his arms to carry her in. He kissed her neck, barely paying attention to where he was going as he walked down a few steps into the main hall. Clara kicked her feet lightly as his lips tickled her skin. He stopped walking and kissed her harder, sucking gently in a way that made her shiver with anticipation. Then, lifting his head, he said, "My lovely bride, may I present—by all that is sacred!" His grip loosened as he jolted in surprise, nearly dropping her.

Clara managed to catch herself upright before she fell on her backside. She followed his gaze upward.

"What is that?" He didn't move.

Clara grinned, seeing a very familiar portrait. "My family. My parents must have sent it as a wedding gift." The large fabric reproduction showcased not only her parents but all of her brothers and sisters. It stretched across the entire side of the main living area, angled from the ceiling so one could easily see it from the floor. The wooden frame had been pieced together like a puzzle to hold the canvas.

"Yes," Vlad said carefully. His expression was unusually blank. "The king did mention your parents honored us with a large gift. I was so preoccupied with the excitement of marrying you that I forgot he said he was sending it to our home for us."

She worried at his tone. "You're disappointed because the proportions are a bit off. I know that each person depicted is smaller than life size, but it is close. I am sure I can request another one, bigger, if you think it is not pleasing as is."

"No, my sweet, sweet wife, not too small at all. It's, ah, perfect." He wrapped his arm about her shoulder and looked up at it, holding her in such a way she couldn't readily see his face.

She felt a small shiver work over his body and started to ask him about it. "Vlad, your tone is strange—"

"I believe your trunks are upstairs," he broke in before she could finish. "Perhaps you should make sure everything is in order."

Clara nodded to do as he suggested. She thought of the space credits and gemstones hidden within her trunks and was slightly amazed she'd forgotten all about them. Open wood steps led up the side wall toward a balcony rail. From above, she could see below until she stepped back into the more private area of the room. A large bed dominated the center of the floor. Polished stone blocks were covered with soft fur rugs. Lights filtered in from above, but the room was still dim. The walls were barren but for a few tapestries and empty sconces. Large floor pillows centered around a triangular fireplace.

It took a moment, but she located an area accessible through an opening in the far wall. From a distance, it gave the illusion of being solid stone, but when she stepped close she found an entire dressing section through an opening. Her trunks were there, as were the bolts of material. She opened the first and found the wig she wore on her wedding day. After the mine, that day felt so long ago. The faint smell of perfume wafted over her when she lifted the heavy piece to set it on the floor. Her smile faded.

Would her parents understand her decision to stay? Would they respect it? Or would they try to force her to return to Redde to have her children? Her opinion of Qurilixen had changed, but how she saw her husband would not be how her parents saw him. She knew the Draig to be honorable, happy people. Her parents would think them overly emotional barbarians, primitives whose only redeeming quality is that they produced male children. But what good were male children to the great lord and lady if they could not raise them in a Redding home?

Stepping back, she held perfectly still and stared at the towering hair. Clara wanted to stay. She knew that unquestioningly. But she also knew when her parents wanted something done, they got it done.

Clara turned her back on the wig, pushing her fears down. Vlad wouldn't let anything happen to her. She trusted in that. Though her parents might try, this was her home and she wasn't going anywhere.

VLAD TRIED NOT to look up at the many eyes staring down at him. The portrait completely dominated the space, giving the feeling of a stoically judging audience inspecting his every move. Now, he wasn't exactly prudish by any sense of the word, but he had a hard time imagining doing the things he wanted to do to his wife with that inexpressive gathering watching on. The banner of his adopted family's dragon standard had been moved to accommodate the piece and now hung over his front door. He could just imagine the laughs as the servants put the monstrosity of a wedding gift up.

Vlad vowed never, ever, *ever*—for the happiness of his marriage—dare to call the portrait a monstrosity out loud. His wife loved it so he would learn to live with it. He glanced up. Every creepy, unamused inch of it.

Though it had been a while since he'd stayed in the fortress home, he wasn't surprised to see it had been cleaned. Without looking, he knew the bathing room to the right would be stocked with soaps and drying linens. His office would be lined with scrolls he rarely acknowledged and reports Mirek liked to write for his brothers—longwinded things that bespoke of his ambassadorial missions in agonizing detail. Too bad Mirek hadn't found a bride at the ceremony. Perhaps then the man would have less time for reporting. Undoubtedly, a new stack rested there untouched since the servants had set them down.

To the right, his kitchen would have basics, including a food simulator he didn't like. As soon as the servants learned he was at home, they would make sure to stock his home with perishables. Hidden inside the wall would be his liquor stash. Actually a drink didn't sound so bad at the moment.

"Vlad?"

He stopped mid-action and turned to the door as it slid open. His brother Alek stepped inside. "Cenek said you had arrived. Now, would you like to explain why we have double the amount of ceffyls milling about outside? They will overrun the pastures within a year if we keep them all here."

"Actually, not at the moment," he answered.

Alek stopped and looked up. He visibly retracted. "What in the name of—?"

"My wife's family," Vlad inserted before his brother could say anything insulting. He pointed to his room where Clara was, letting Alek know they were not alone. Loudly, he added, "Isn't it a lovely gift."

Alek made a weak noise and nodded his head. Just as loud, but not very convincingly, he said, "Yes, lovely."

"I hear you and Bron have found wives," Vlad said. "Many blessings, brother."

Alek's face softened and Vlad could tell his brother had been blessed with a well-made match. "Mirek too. There was some confusion as to his luck because she was not in the traditional receiving line. Actually, his luck now is…"

"Is she…?" Vlad prompted, willing Alek to continue his comment about Mirek's bride.

Alek looked up and gave a small frown. With his hands, he gestured first to the painting and then above his head to indicate all the women had cone-shaped heads in the portrait. He pointed up to Vlad's room. Silently, he mouthed, "Is she…?"

Vlad grimaced and shook his head in denial.

Alek gave a dramatic, soundless sigh of relief. Vlad very happily punched him. Hard.

Alek laughed. "I deserve that."

"What about Mirek's luck?" Vlad prompted, trying to draw his brother's gaze off the portrait.

"Lady Riona, his wife, is in stasis. Mirek had an isolation chamber built for her. We've had the Medical Alliance doctors here but they're not sure why she won't wake up. After their ceremony was completed, Mirek found her in a patch of the yellow. The doctors said she's not contagious and she doesn't carry any known alien diseases."

The yellow was a low-growing, ground-covering

plant near the palace whose spores induced tempo-rary sleep. Though fatal in long doses if the victim happened to never wake up and thus starved to death, its affects generally wore off quickly once a person stopped breathing it in. It wasn't known to cause prolonged illnesses, especially none that required physicians and isolation.

"I've never heard if it making a person sleep for so long, but they think it might have been an allergic reaction," Alek finished. "As luck would have it, Bron married Riona's sister, Lady Aeron, so the sleeping lady is well cared for."

Vlad didn't doubt Mirek would ensure every comfort for his ill bride. He couldn't imagine the worry his brother must be feeling.

"It's you!" Clara's cheeks were slightly flushed as she came down the stairs. She'd wound her hair to the nape of her neck, keeping it off her face. Vlad automatically smiled to see her. She stepped past him as she studied Alek's face.

"My lady," Alek said, bowing his head. "You recognize me without my mask?"

"Solarflowers," she stated, as if that one thought needed to explode out of her body. "Please, for my sanity, give the ceffyls solarflowers."

"My lady?" Alek glanced at Vlad in question, clearly not following.

"They won't leave me alone. They follow me

around. They keep showing me pictures of you catching babies that do not make it. I think they mourn because then they keep insisting they need to eat solarflowers. At this point, if I have to grow them myself, I will. But please. Solarflowers."

"My lady...?" Alek gestured to her while turning to Vlad. "Is she...well?"

"Quite," Vlad said. He waited a few more seconds, enjoying Alek's helpless confusion before finally explaining his wife's gifts and her communication with the beasts. Clara stood beside him nodding as he spoke.

"That is a remarkable gift, my lady," Alek said. "I will take your words under advisement."

Clare sighed heavily in relief. "Thank you, my lord." Vlad began to speak when Clara suddenly stiffened. Her eyes darkened, ringing with green. "We have to go. Your brother is in danger. They put him underground."

"What are you...?" Vlad touched her arm.

She blinked several times before grabbing him. "The Tyoe. That is what I couldn't see earlier because the ceffyls kept insisting. But the Tyoe put your brother underground. They hope to distract you all into looking for him. They keep him alive in case they need to move him or use him. But he's trapped."

"She does have a gift," Alek put forth in

shock. "That already happened. Bron was captured in the forest and left chained in this underground prison near the hunting cabin. The Var seemed the more likely culprit at the time, though we are so far north from the borderlands and could not detect their *cat-shifter* stink in the forest. However, since we didn't recall there being an old underground prison in the forest, I have to assume the cell is a relic of the ancient wars. The Var most likely would have no way of knowing of the prison's existence. Lady Aeron told us she intercepted a transmission saying aliens calling themselves Tyoe might try to take our mines by force."

"Is Bron harmed? What happened?" Vlad demanded, wondering why no one had sent for him.

"It was over quickly. I found him and he is safe," Alek assured him. "Mirek has just recently returned from space. He scanned the sky, or did whatever those ships of his do, and determined that an alien craft was recently over the mountains, but whoever it was has left. Precautions are being taken to ensure our protection. The king has ordered we take care of the matter. He has enough problems with King Attor. The Var have been crossing into our territory and he worries there will be a war before the princes properly settle their marriages."

He turned to Clara. "How did you know about the Tyoe's plan?"

Vlad told the story of the mine and what his wife had done.

A subtle shift came over Alek's expression, and by the time Vlad had finished, his brother lifted a hand to Clara's shoulders. He nodded once in full approval of her. "Well done." Then, hooking her about the shoulders, Alek didn't give them an option but to follow him as he added, "Now come meet the rest of your family, my lady. I am sure they will want to hear of this. But I warn you, Lady Aeron is with child and you do not want to reach between her and a plate of Lithorian chocolates. She nearly bit my hand off."

"Wonderful," Clara said, turning to smile at Vlad. "The first of her twenty."

Alek opened his mouth to inquire but Vlad shook his head. "No, brother, don't ask."

15

CLARA PEERED through the thick clear door to the isolation chamber where Lady Riona slept. The woman was covered in red blisters and kept under constant medical monitoring in the sterile room. The auburn length of her hair was twisted on the top of her head into a very neat, very plain bun. Clara was used to seeing people in stasis because of her sisters. Nothing about the thick yellow tubes inserted into the body and fine white powder covering the patchy skin was pretty, but the woman should be in a comfortable sleep.

Lord Mirek was not at home but his emotion output told Clara he derived comfort from others stopping to visit his bride, so Clara did her duty and came every day to stand quietly by the door.

Mirek's section of the mountain home had smoothed stone floors, thick rugs and oversized wood furniture. Couches were arranged in a square around a low table with a center fire pit. It was comfortable compared to the cold sterility of Lady Riona's current room.

"I hope to meet you soon, Lady Riona," Clara said softly, lifting her hand before her face to project a greeting to the woman. Like always, Lady Riona did not move, and Clara doubted the lady knew what she said to her.

The last several weeks in the castle home had been interesting as the new family tried to get to know each other. Lord Bron was the High Duke and his wife, Lady Aeron, was a communication specialist who oversaw the installation of communication upgrades. Lord Alek often called Clara to the pasture to speak to the ceffyls. She hated to go but thought it her duty to help when called upon. Clara didn't complain. In some ways, she was still the lady her mother raised her to be. Alek's wife, Lady Kendall, had a brilliant scientist's mind. She spoke to Mirek and Vlad about the ore mines in a way that gave Clara a slight ache in her head. Though, despite Kendall's frequent mentions of *galaxa-promethium*, Clara liked her well enough.

There could be little doubt that the Draig men loved their wives. The brothers' emotions radiated off of them every time the women were near. The wives returned the sentiment wholeheartedly—well, except for Riona who probably didn't know Mirek was even there. It filled Clara with love to be around them as a group. It was a feeling missing from her childhood. Clara had no doubt she'd been loved, but it had not been shown as it was here. When she had her children, they would know love. The thought warmed her heart.

"Clara?"

Clara turned to the door. The smiles came to her face more naturally now, though her new sisters-by-marriage confessed her moods were hard to read. Aeron crossed over to the room to look in on her sister. A wave of sadness emitted from the woman.

"I was just leaving," Clara said. "I will give you privacy."

"No, I can't stay. I was actually asked to find you and bring you to your section of the castle." Aeron touched the glass door lightly before turning to walk Clara from the home.

"Has something happened? Vlad should not be back until morning."

Soon after their arrival at the castle, Lord Bron had sent an army into the mines to look for aliens. Reports also came that the fracking fluid was being cleaned up the best the Draig miners could manage and the hollow would soon be sealed. There would be no mining until the workers were safe. They'd even had to cancel their annual mining festival to deal with the immediate threats. Vlad had traveled down to the mines several times in the last weeks and Clara hated it when he left. However, there was a connection between them, stronger than anything she'd ever experienced, and she could feel him inside her no matter the distance. If he were in danger, she would know.

"I know not. I suppose Mirek might have more news from space?" Aeron frowned. "Or perhaps the men are back from the mountains early?"

Clara closed her eyes and took a deep breath. "I don't think so."

"I managed to pick up some old Earth transmissions when I was up in the tower installing a new communication node." Aeron walked with her through the quiet halls. They passed a few servants. "I'm recording what I can. We might be missing a little of the transmission, but if you'd like to join us, Kendall and I are going to have some girls only time. We'll be hiding in my husband's old home where the men won't look for us."

They reached Clara's home and she nodded, hovering her hand over the scanner. "I would love to."

"I told the servant to bring me Lady Clara of the Redding, not two more servants."

Clara stiffened. A familiar perfume surrounded her.

"Clara?" Aeron whispered.

Clara turned wide eyes to find her parents standing in the middle of her Draig home. Their dispassionate faces gave nothing away as they stared at her.

The great lord was immaculate, from his powdered wig to his long jacket. Jaene was just as ornate with a pink gown encrusted with green gemstones, wide hoop skirt and a tall wig that was nearly half the woman's natural height. Her mother's face was paled by cosmetics, expect for the bright pink lips and cheeks, and green lashes and brows.

The couple matched, which only made Clara feel all the more out of place. Clara took a deep breath and then another before locking eyes with them. They both looked at her, not realizing who she was. No wonder. Decorum had many rules, and Clara currently was breaking most of them.

"You should leave," she whispered to Aeron. The woman looked as if she might protest, but in the end she did as Clara indicated.

Clara drew the expression from her face and stoically made her way forward. She lifted her wrist to her mother. "Welcome to my new home, Great Lady."

Her mother stood, unmoving, simply staring at her unpainted face. Clara turned to her father and lifted her wrist. Before she could finish the gesture, he snapped, "What dishonor is this? You dare to greet us dressed like a commoner? I thought you a servant."

Clara drew her eyes to the floor. "Forgive me, Great Lord, for my appearance." She felt like a child again, only worse. Out of all the things she'd done, of the times she dared to question them or acted even slightly contrary, she had never broken as many Redding customs as she did on this planet. She thought when she saw them she wouldn't care about traditions, instead showing them how happy she was in her marriage. Instead, one smell of her mother's perfume, two disapproving looks and she was reduced to what she was raised to be—their noble daughter…who was currently disappointing them.

"What did I tell you when you left?" her mother demanded.

Clara recited the words, "Remember the lady I have raised you to be. You represent all of your family with each action you take. I mourn your going, but rejoice in the next generation."

"And yet your hair is loose and your skin is

naked," Jaene said. "Did the barbarians take your cosmetics?"

Clara thought of the young boys who'd thought her cosmetics were war paint. She started to chuckle. Her mother's gasp stopped her and she dropped her head lower.

"Monitor yourself," her mother demanded in a flat tone that was edged with hardness.

"Forgive me, Great Lady, for my new home's customs," Clara said in a docile tone. "I am only acting as the Great Lord of the Redding and the Emperor decreed and embracing the culture of my husband's people. This is how noblewomen are expected to appear on this planet."

"Do not be contrary to your mother, Clara," her father asserted.

"Forgive me, Great Lord, for displeasing you," she apologized yet again. Inside, a heavy sensation began to fill her. It left her a little sick to her stomach. She knew they disapproved of her and she was unable to say anything that would make them understand her new life—a life they had sent her to. "Has the new generation started?"

"All female," the great lord answered. "Not the best start to a new line."

Jaene lifted her hand and hovered it over Clara's stomach. After a few moments, she said, "Perhaps this one will be male, Great Lord."

Clara looked at her stomach. A baby? Vlad's baby? Excitement filled her and it was very hard for her to keep it down. Luckily, the nobles were more focused on themselves than their daughter, and they missed the jittery fluttering in her chest.

News of her condition seemed to brighten her father some. "Then our timing is well planned, Great Lady."

Clara wondered why she had never noticed the stilted way her parents spoke to each other. She thought of Arianwen and her sons. She thought of their laughter and warmth.

Her father continued, "When your mother told me of what your companion reported to her, I knew we must come as soon as it was convenient for us to do so."

"All that beautiful material wasted on the floor." Jaene gave a single shake of her head. "When I heard about the ruined bolts, I wished I had forced you to take the Emperor's confidant, Lord Camern. Then the Emperor would not have been so angry and insisted you come here to these barbarians."

Clara lifted her gaze. That was the first she'd heard of this being an actual punishment. Before she could think to stop it, she said, "Lord Camern is in love with himself."

"Monitor!" her mother fervently whispered.

They still stood in the middle of the room.

Clara realized her parents thought themselves above sitting on the Draig furniture.

"In such a short time, these primitives have done so much damage. I mourn the loss of my hard work." The great lady shared a stoic look with her husband. "They have even taken her proper gowns and dressed her in this rag."

Clara looked at the gown Arianwen had made for her after the mine collapse. She rather liked the ornate stitches along the sleeves. Seeing Jaene's expressionless face, she wondered what her mother would think about Clara being trapped in a mine, alone with several men for days, eating spiders.

"And why is our family portrait on the floor?" Jaene gestured behind her.

"My lord husband has decided to respect the Redde tradition and is building a portrait hall where this is being moved. It will be the first hung in a position of honor." Clara thought it a very sweet gesture by her husband. He seemed very proud of the idea, so she didn't tell him she thought the eyes of her family staring at her when she kissed him was odd as well. Let him think he had that one secret.

"We will take her home now," her father decided.

"As you wish, always as you wish," Jaene agreed. "I will manage the problem and ensure your grandchild is not primitive. I will not have my daughter without noble refinements. I believe this is enough punishment. Though, perhaps you would wish that I redress her here, before we are seen by the crew?"

"That is what I so commanded," the great lord answered, though he had said no such thing. "If the barbarians try to stop us, we'll send armies to destroy them."

The way he said it was so simple and matter of fact, as if he commented that the sky on Qurilixen was green.

"As you wish, husband, always as you wish," Jaene said, never disagreeing with her husband's words. Finally, as her parents' will was decided, her mother lifted her hand to Clara in a loving gesture. Clara felt comfort in those thin blue veins, pale skin and fragrant perfume, but it was merely the comfort of a fond childhood memory. Without touching her daughter's disagreeably naked face, Jaene let the gesture drop.

Clara instinctively repeated the movement with her own wrist to her mother. This had been the plan from the beginning. Come to Qurilixen, marry, become pregnant and then go home. She had done all they had sent her to do. When she looked at their expectant expressions, she knew she'd been a fool to think she would ever be allowed to stay with Vlad, no matter how much she loved him. Duty did not care about love. Her parents did not care what her heart wanted. She had no doubt her father would send his armies to take her by force if she tried to stay without their blessing. She had no wish for others to die on her behalf.

As she looked at them, her face became the stoic mask they would expect in their daughter. She stiffened her body and mimicked their statuesque poses. The gesture came easier now that she'd accepted her place.

"It will be as you wish," Clara said, using every bit of strength she had not to cry. "But I have one condition that must first be met before we can go."

VLAD GROWLED as the castle finally came into view. He'd been running for nearly an hour in shifted form, trying to get home. Something was not right. His heart felt as if it was being torn from his chest. Clara had been a constant inside him and then suddenly, without warning, she'd disappeared. Though his muscles burned and his lungs heaved for air, he pushed harder.

He followed his instincts down the center hall to the common rooms. Grabbing the corner edge of the wall to propel himself on, he slid to a stop at the scroll room door. A light gasp sounded but he ignored it. His eyes desperately sought Clara, and he sighed with relief when he found that she was there and she was well. Then he noticed her tall wig and painted face. She sat still, perched on the end of a wide chair. The furniture accommodated her wide skirt.

The slow exhaling of breath was hardly notice-able to human hearing, but his dragon senses detected it easily. Next to his wife was an older Redde woman. Her eyes were wide and her lips parted. Though her face was devoid of any true emotion, he knew by the sound of her frantically beating heart he terrified her. By her face, he knew she was Clara's mother. Vlad instantly shifted to human form and stepped forward.

"My apologies, I did not mean to frighten you," he said. "You must be Clara's mother, Lady Redding."

"Lady Jaene, the Great Lady of the Redding," Jaene corrected tersely. He recognized that tone. It was the exact same tone Clara had used at their wedding ceremony to correct him.

"Lady Jaene," Vlad acknowledged. He found himself standing taller in response to their rigid positioning. He glanced questioningly at his wife, expecting a smile from her. Her eyes met his very briefly before she turned them forward and stared ahead.

"I am Lady Clara's father, the Great Lord of the Redding," a man said. Vlad had not seen him standing in the corner when he entered. He turned and bowed his head politely. For some reason, he felt like a scolded child when the man looked at him. "You may address me as Great Lord. My wife is Great Lady."

"Great Lord." Vlad bowed his head again, feeling somewhat compelled to formality. "I am Lord Vladan, Ealdorman Honorary of the Draig, High Mining Official."

"So my daughter informed me," the great lord said. He looked down his nose at Vlad, studying him. "She did not, however," he gave Clara a dispassionate glance, "inform me you were a shifter."

"I am sure she was respecting our planet's custom of not sharing the fact with off-worlders that we are dragon-shifters." Vlad reached his feelings out and tried to silently get a sense of his wife's emotions, but he detected nothing. She blocked herself from him. He didn't like this.

The man nodded, accepting this answer. "This will certainly bring new blood to our line." He looked at his wife. "We will have to reconsider our position." Jaene nodded once in agreement.

"Clara, you will be required to have more than the child you now carry."

"Pregnant?" Vlad grinned. He suddenly didn't care about his parent-by-marriage's stuffy customs. He went to his wife and knelt at her feet. "Is it true? A baby?"

Clara tried not to look at him. He saw her bottom lip tremble. A thin bead of moisture gathered along her bottom lashes but did not spill over. After several deep breaths, she said, "My father has agreed to speak to the Tyoe ambassador. They will not bother your people again, my lord husband. If they do, my father has pledged his Redde army to come and defeat them with their very presence. The Tyoe will not risk angering him."

"Clara?" he whispered. Why wouldn't she look at him? What was wrong with her?

"Do get off the floor," the great lord demanded.

Vlad didn't readily obey. However, when it became apparent Clara was not going to look at him, he slowly rose to his feet. What was he not understanding? What had they done to his wife?

"It is as my daughter says," the great lord continued only when Vlad was standing fixedly before him. "We sent her here to marry. Duty dictates we honor your connection to our family and provide aid should your planet need it. Clara has called upon us to honor that duty. The Tyoe are easy-enough foes. They will bend to my will, as most foes do."

"Then on behalf of my people, I thank you for your interference. We will fight, but avoiding war and the loss of life is always preferable. I knew there was reason the gods blessed me with such a fine wife." Vlad tried very hard to hide his irritation. Oh, but he was irritated. This man was insufferable and arrogant and…what in the known universes had they done to his wife? He should be swinging her in circles, screaming to the heavens his good fortune over the new baby. Instead, he felt like the character in some strange play, acting as someone other than himself. "The gods sent Lady Clara to me to—"

"I sent Lady Clara to marry a nobleman," the great lord corrected.

"It is their culture, Great Lord," Clara said softly. "Here the gods are everywhere."

The great lord nodded in understanding but did not apologize.

"My daughter has requested a moment with you before we are to leave," the great lord said.

"You are not staying?" Even as he offered, Vlad was somewhat relieved. The fact they were Clara's parents made him feel guilty about it. "I can have the servants prepare a wing for you. It is decorated for a High Duke."

"No," was all the great lord said. He reached his arm to his wife, hooking it to help her to her feet. The heavy weight of her gown swung around her before settling. She nodded at him and followed her husband from the room.

Clara held her arm like her mother had. Vlad hooked it and helped her up. He smiled now they were alone. "Is it true, sweet wife? A baby?" He moved as if to grab her face to kiss her.

She shook her head and pulled back. Clara put distance between them. "When my father said we were leaving, he meant *we*. I'm going with them."

Vlad furrowed his brow and balled his fists. "They're not taking you away. You're my wife, Clara. You love me. I don't know what kind of drug they put in that war paint of yours, but you do love me. If I have to scrub you down myself I will, but you love me."

Clara inhaled a shaky breath. "Vlad, please, don't." Her will slipped and he felt inside her. She did love him and her heart was breaking. He tried to touch her and she again stepped away from him, this time putting furniture between them.

"Clara, you can't go," he pleaded.

"DON'T MAKE THIS HARDER."

Clara wanted nothing more than to throw her arms around round Vlad and hold him forever. When she'd agreed to go with her parents to please them in exchange for their help with the Tyoe, she'd known it would be hard, but she never thought it would be this difficult. Inside, she felt her heart thundering in her chest. Outside, she had to project calm. If she looked at him for too long all would be lost. Her father would be angered by her display.

"I don't understand." His face tightened.

"My father agreed to…" She sniffed, trying very hard not to cry.

"He thinks we're beneath him," Vlad concluded. "He sent you here to marry a nobleman so he could have his grandchildren and, now that you're pregnant, has come to gather you to the family fold. Does he really think I'm just going to stand by and let this happen? Does he think I'm going to let him take my wife and my son?"

"It is not that simple," she protested.

"It is that simple, Clara. You belong with me." Vlad made a move to come for her. She ventured around the chair, keeping it between them.

"It is the only way. You saw what happened when there was only one Tyoe worker. What do you think will happen when their soldiers come?

MICHELLE M. PILLOW

They already kidnapped the High Duke without detection. They have invaded your mines. One nearly killed you." The tear fell and she tried to dab it back so it wouldn't ruin her face and upset her parents. "This is why your gods called me here. You said it yourself. Our marriage has made an alliance possible. The Redding army can easily defeat the Tyoe. They do not even need to march. They just have to exist. If I stay I will risk watching you die, watching everyone I have come to care about die—Ari and Tomos and Sven and Matus and Nolan, Aeron and Bron, Alek and Kendall, Riona and—"

"I wasn't lying when I told your father we would fight the Tyoe if we had to," Vlad said. "We are not cowards."

"I know. You are all so strong and brave, but you also said this was the best way—to end a war before its starts without loss of life."

"Then I will go with you," Vlad said.

Clara gasped. "You would leave everything for...?" She couldn't ask him to do that, but knowing he loved her that much caused her to shake. "No, I—"

"Lady Clara."

Clara blinked, seeing her mother. She sniffed. "The great lord told me I'd have more time than this. Please—"

"Monitor yourself," her mother warned. Clara nodded, dabbing at her eyes.

Vlad took the opportunity to hop over the chair to stand next to Clara. He wrapped his arm around her shoulders and pulled her next to him. "I'm coming with you."

Jaene's brows furrowed ever so slightly and Clara knew her mother would be horrified by the idea of a barbarian in her home.

"I have spoken to your father." Jaene glanced down the hall before stepping inside the room. Clara assumed her father waited in the hall out of sight to listen. Had they been eavesdropping on her talk with her husband? "It is apparent this planet needs more assistance than just a Redding army. There will be no reason to save it if it is not worth saving."

Vlad started to move forward in offense. Clara hooked his elbow and squeezed her arm tightly against his to stop him.

Jaene focused her attention on her son-by-marriage. "Do you think our titles are merely shells? A key to position and power so that we may frolic at will? I can tell by looking at you that you were not born to nobility. No true nobleman would act as you do. However, it is of no consequence how you came to the title, it is yours. I will explain to you as I did to my sons when they were children and I had to separate them from playing with the lower class servants. You are a lord, Vladan. The men who serve you do not need a friend. They need a leader. That is your burden and your duty. Do not be reluctant. Do not hesitate. Take your place, Lord Vladan, Ealdorman Honorary of the Draig, High Mining Official. Yes, we as nobles have privileges, but we also have responsibilities. We make sacrifices. It is your duty to behave accordingly."

Vlad didn't answer. Clara stepped toward her mother. "Wise words, Great Lady."

"Remember then to tell your son of his expected duties when he is born," she directed.

"Will you not be there to tell him?" Clara asked, trying to keep the hope from her voice.

"You always did have overly expressive eyes," her mother lectured. "Your father wishes that you should stay here and instruct these barbarians. He sees the wisdom in it. If we are to connect our name to this planet, at least one true Redding should be here to oversee our interest." She gave a pointed look to Vlad. "Besides, as your family, we will gratefully receive your gifts of ore."

And there it was. What her father thought more valuable than bringing a daughter home. Ore to fuel his ships.

"Our pleasure," Vlad said, easily accepting the terms of her proposed bribe.

Clara knew that this change was her mother's doing. The great lady would have mentioned the wisdom to her father who'd then taken the idea as his own.

Clara nodded. She tried to fight her emotions but it was hard. "Thank you, Mother," she whispered.

"It is as your father wishes," the great lady said. She lifted her hand toward her daughter.

Clara couldn't resist. She leaned forward and wrapped her arms around her mother, letting her feel all the love and gratitude inside her. Their wigs bumped. Jaene stiffened and didn't move. Their heavy dresses pressed tightly together, catching a little when Clara pulled away.

Her mother opened her mouth and then closed it several times. Her words were low, as she said, "Never do that again."

"As my mother wishes," Clara said.

Jaene shook her head once. "You always did have expressive eyes. Fear not the Tyoe. Your father goes to the ship now to hail their ambassador."

"Thank you, Great Lady," Clara said, lifting her wrist. This gesture was much more familiar to the woman and her mother lifted her wrist as well, not touching.

When she left, Clara turned to her husband, grinning. "Apparently you are so in need of my help that I am being forced to stay here."

"If you think I'm wearing a powdered wig you are…well, I will if it makes you happy." He took a step toward her. "Do you need to tell them goodbye?"

"It was implied."

"So much for you to teach me about being noble." Vlad's impish grin said he had no intention of trying to be a Redding gentleman. She very, very much agreed with him on that point. Clara wanted her dragon just the way he was.

"You heard my mother. Though we are noble, that does not mean we must live horrible lives." She moved a little toward him, carefully balancing in her stiff boots. "I do fear you will need much training."

He arched a brow. Her gown kept her from getting too close to him. He leaned forward so their lips could meet to softly brush.

"You showed me how to laugh. Let me show you how to be my nobleman," she whispered before drawing back slightly. "But first maybe help me out of this hair? I feel like I'm going to tip over."

"As my wife wishes," he murmured. He held his arm out for her to hook hers through and began to escort her back to their room. Then, grinning, he added, "If we hurry, maybe I can get you pregnant with twins."

Clara chuckled. "Ah, husband, I don't think that is how these things work."

"Still, I would definitely like to try."

EPILOGUE

"HUSBAND." Clara ran her hand over her rounded belly as her husband massaged her feet.

"Wife?"

"You were saying something to me on our wedding night in that dragon tongue of yours. What was it?" She wiggled her toes when his hands paused.

"I said many things to you that night." He lifted her bare foot to place kisses on it. "And I wanted to do much more to you, beautiful temptress."

Clara pulled her foot from him and leaned over on their couch so she could press her face into his neck. She knew he liked it when she kissed him there. "It was something you said your father used to say to your mother, but you never told me what it meant."

Vlad tossed back his head and began to laugh.

"What?" She withdrew.

"Hope I'm not interrupting." Alek strode in as the door slid open. He had his hands over his eyes.

"You are, go away," Vlad demanded playfully with a growl.

"I have to speak to…" Alek pulled his hand down to peek. Seeing them on the couch fully clothed, he hurried to Clara. "I know what they were trying to tell you. I was thinking of the images, and it's the solarflowers. They——"

"No," Clara moaned. "Not the solarflowers again. Come back tomorrow. I have no wish to talk to ceffyls today."

"No, the lost babies. They're trying to tell us the solarflowers help the pregnancy. I put three expectant mares who were close to their times on a solarflower diet. They were happy, they were active and they all just had healthy babies. We'll have to wean them off it, but it worked. Solarflowers." Alek gave a little dance of excitement. "I've ordered seeds harvested at once. We'll begin planting a crop in a few months. But do you know what this means? No more fifty-percent chance of a live birth."

Clara gave him a serious look. "Have you told your wife this news?"

Alek looked shocked for a moment. "No, I haven't."

"I'm sure she'd love to hear all about it," Clara stated. "You should go find her at once."

"You're right!" Alek hurried from the room.

"Kendall might not appreciate that," Vlad teased.

Clara leaned for him. "Now, husband, don't think I forgot. What did you say to me on our wedding night?"

Vlad held his lips near hers. For a moment, she thought he might try to get out of answering. Then, a second before their mouths touched, he admitted, "It translates to *my solarflower*."

The End

The series continues with Dragon Lords: The Impatient Lord.

THE SERIES CONTINUES...

Need more Dragon Lords?
The books continue!
Dragon Lords 8: The Impatient Lord

Want to see how the King and Queen met?
Dragon Lords 9: The Dragon's Queen

Want to see how King Attor's sons turn out,
despite their father's teachings?
Lords of the Var®: The Savage King

Read all the Dragon Lords and Var books?
Yay, you, keep going!

Space Lords 1: His Frost Maiden

Dragon Lords and *Lords of the Var*®
in Modern Day Earth?

Captured by a Dragon-Shifter: Determined Prince

THE IMPATIENT LORD

DRAGON LORDS 8

Dragon-shifter Romance
by Michelle M. Pillow

An unlucky bride...

Riona Grey lives life on her own terms, traveling wherever the next spaceship is flying and doing what she must in order to get by. When her luck turns sour, she finds herself on a bridal ship heading to a marriage ceremony. A planet full of dragon-shifters seeking mates wasn't exactly what she had in mind as a final destination. Just when she thinks things couldn't possibly get worse, she wakes up months later in an isolation chamber with a sexy, hovering dragon-shifter by her side telling her they're meant to be together... forever.

The impatient groom...

After years of failed marriage attempts at the Breeding Festivals, the gods finally revealed Lord Mirek's bride...a day too late. Eager to have her, he defied tradition and laid claim. But it is a mistake to go against the gods and his new wife was the one to pay the price of his impatience.

Now almost a year later, his bride is finally waking from her deep sleep. With one look from her, he feels the eagerness to claim her overtaking him once more. Fearful she'll slip through his grasp once again, he's hesitant to anger the gods by taking her to his bed too soon. But, how can he resist the one thing that would make his life complete, especially when she looks at him with eyes of a seductress? This is one test he can't fail, and yet with one of her sweet kisses he knows he may already have lost.

First Chapter Excerpt

Intergalactic Gambling Championship, Torgan Black Market
City of Madaga, Planet of Torgan

Riona Grey knew better than to press her luck. Unfortunately, that didn't stop her from opening her mouth to issue perhaps the stupidest challenge she'd ever uttered, "Oh, I know I can win, Range. I'm the best. I could beat your guys blindfolded, after a night spent hallucinating on Torganian Rum and drunk off my ass. In fact, I can take this whole tournament."

Of course, the space pirate had to force her to put her money where her mouth was because she'd said it in front of his entire crew. And, of course, Riona took his bet and tripled it because, well, she was a sucker for high stakes and mischief. Besides, every time Range crossed her path, he pissed her off. He didn't really do anything, but his smarmy, sexist nature rubbed her the wrong way. She saw his smug face and she wanted to hit him. Instead, she continued on to insult his manhood, his ship and, perhaps most wounding of all, his reputation as a space pirate. Apparently, pirate captains didn't like to be called, "second-rate cargo shippers with a puffed-up reputation with only a list of misdemeanor planetary level charges to his credit." That one got a gun pointed in her face and the ante upped to nearly four times the original amount—fifty-thousand space credits.

Good thing she was an expert when it came to gambling, because she didn't have that kind of money.

Good thing she was so close to winning.

Range could lick her boots. It was going to be

sweet perfection to see his face as he handed over that many space credits. Adding that to the tournament prizes and she'd be set for life. No more running around taking odd jobs and doing whatever she could to survive. This was it. Her chance.

The tournament was a lock. There was no way she was losing at Frendle's Chips. This was her game. She would walk away with the winnings, an extra fifty-thousand space credits and some of Range's pride. Today was going to be a good day. Looking up at the glass-and-metal ceiling, she quietly corrected herself, "Tonight is going to be a *great* night." Traveling from planet to planet, living in deep space, it became hard to differentiate night from day. Really, it just depended on where you landed.

Riona loved her life. She loved everything about it. Well, almost everything, but she had seen enough to know better than to complain. Things could always be worse. She could still be starving, fighting for a small corner of a ship so that she could sleep undisturbed. Desperation and necessity had taught her how to survive, and she was good at it. There were no handouts in the universe for people like her.

The loud music, smoky atmosphere and drunken patrons were comforting in their familiarity. She liked how simplistic everyone was on this level of existence. The humanoid and non-humanoid aliens were predictable. They could be expected to uphold certain codes of honor…to a point. They would act in their own self-interest first, the interest of their crew second, and in the interest of breaking the law third.

There was freedom to their tarnished honor. But best of all, none of them had any grand plans beyond amassing more money and having more adventures. They had flown to the ends of the known universes and had seen marvels beyond speech, and yet living creatures in general still managed to debase that beauty. For most of them, life was short and fairly pointless. Disasters happened. Ships exploded. Fortunes were lost. Planets were blown into nothingness. And sometimes, smarmy pirates lost bets to a girl.

Riona smiled at her last opponent, feeling her heartbeat quicken. One play left. That's all she needed. One perfect play and she walked away the tournament winner. She was aware of the stares of those in the complex on her, knew her face was being broadcast in an oversized holographic projection floating above her head so everyone could see. Long, metal tables stretched out before her, most of them occupied with spectators. The smell of liquor exuded from the nearby bar that dominated the center of the building. Smoke filtered along the floor, being drawn to ventilation grates.

Riona reached to the table next to her and made a show of taking an unconcerned drink. In truth, she could barely swallow because her heart was beating so hard. Metal discs floated before her in a large game grid. Tiny snaps of electricity shot between them. She tapped her fingernails against an inert disc as she contemplated her next move. Her mind raced and calculated, making sense of the seemingly random pattern of electrical shocks.

"I hear human women often freeze under pressure," her opponent jeered. He talked in his native language of Yidie, but she understood the scaly lizard man just fine thanks to her implanted universal translator.

Riona laughed a loud, delighted sound as she held up her disc. To herself, she quietly counted, *One, Two, Thr*—

"Ri!"

At the sudden, startling sound, her fingers slipped and the disc went a millimeter off its original course and right into a strip of electricity. For the longest second, her heart stopped beating and her confident smile fell. The unit blinked once and then fizzled as the disc was destroyed. Metal particles fell to the table. Chaos erupted in a series of cheers and pounding fists of protest.

Turning almost numbly to the distraction, she had to blink to be sure she wasn't seeing things. Aeron? What in all the bounty of Jareth was her sister doing here? Now?

Unable to believe her eyes, she stood, consciously forcing the smile back to her lips. She couldn't appear too shaken, not with fifty-thousand space credits now past due and a collector only too willing for an excuse to punish her for reneging. Not to mention it had taken all her savings to enter the tournament. She was now dead broke and in debt to a pirate.

Lights flashed around them and Aeron ducked her head down to avoid the photographs. She wore the uniformed cap of the Federation Military to hide her black hair. A quick glance down told Riona that Aeron also wore the rest of the get-up. Full military blacks. Why in all the fire surges of Bravon was the military here? And why was her sister the analyst with them?

Eyeing Aeron, Riona said through tight lips, "Greetings, sister. I didn't know the Federation was sending security guards to the event. You should have sent a transmission warning me. I would have told you this wasn't your scene."

"I need to talk to you," Aeron said. Nearly five years since she'd seen the woman in the flesh and it was straight to business. Sure, they had the regular, mandatory family communications, but they didn't seek each other out. In fact, it wouldn't surprise Riona if she learned Aeron denied they were related.

"So serious. Careful, it will wrinkle your face." Riona glanced at her lost game before turning her attention to the last place she'd seen Range and his crew. He was easy to spot with his spiky black hair and dark green facial tattoos scrolled along his cheekbones. The pirate grinned at her and lifted his fingers to wave. Sarcastically, she muttered, "Your timing is as impeccable as always."

"This is bigger than playtime. It's serious," Aeron insisted.

"I can see that," Riona said. Range rested his hand on his gun in warning.

"Would you forget about that stupid game? I need you to come with me. This is important. When was the last time I actually came to you for help?" Aeron did have a point. "You know I wouldn't be here if I had any other choice."

"Where are the other militants?" Riona's expression gave nothing away. She couldn't help but wonder if this was a trap. Had her sister come to arrest her? She was with the ship that had hijacked the cold-storage shipment heading toward Harn, but that had been over four years ago. She'd covered her tracks, hadn't she? There was also that

Grooten misunderstanding. Or the bar fight on Valor 6. And she did steal fuel once from a fueling dock on a dare, but she'd been in disguise and the wanted issue had her drawn up to look like a Liphobian sea slug with fur. As far as she could tell, no such creatures actually existed—unless by some horrific misfortune a snowbeast had mated with a Liphobian.

"I'm alone."

"You're here on leave? You left the floating base to actually take a trip?" For a brief second, Riona thought perhaps her sister had actually learned to loosen the belt straps and have a good time.

"Yes, or I was on leave until… Well, no, not exactly, but once I explain you'll realize I didn't have a choice. This is about—"

Riona lifted her hand to stop her sister from explaining and nodded. The people around them might be pretending to party, but she would bet at least five of them listened to the conversation. In fact, several of them might even get ideas. Those who placed wagers on her wouldn't be too happy at Aeron's interruption. Several of them might go so far as to recoup their losses at the cost of her sister's delicate hide.

"Is this favor off planet?" Riona asked. *Blast the stars*. What was she going to do? She'd been so close.

Fifty. Thousand. Space credits.

Riona found it hard to breathe.

"Yes, but it—"

"Do you have a ship?" Riona interrupted, keeping her voice low. She needed to get off this planet and fast. Range would only hold back for so long.

"Yes."

"Then lead the way. You are family after all." Riona lifted a couple of fingers to Range, motioning that she was going to get his money. He narrowed his eyes, but he didn't immediately move to stop her. She knew he would send men to follow her. He trusted her about as much as she trusted him—and with good reason, she was planning on running out on him without paying. "Who am I to disappoint family?"

Aeron tried to stop walking when Riona would usher her through the crowd. "I have a ship that can get us off planet, but—"

"Yeah, yeah, tell me all about it in flight, sis. We'll have plenty of time to catch up in space." Riona tried not to think about her massive loss. She felt the eyes of the crowd on them, watching. It took all her concentration to smile and act unconcerned.

The crowd was the usual mix of disreputable lowlife creatures one would expect to find in

Madaga. Riona knew to stay away from the hired guns and slave traders. However, the pirates, bounty hunters and crooked business men made for decent enough conversation. Though she doubted Aeron would feel the same way. Her sister jerked away from a group of aliens. They looked mostly human but with thick ridges across their foreheads and cheeks. They fanned their webbed hands in front of their faces to create a breeze in the crowded area.

A set of three very hostile eyes met hers. The Pha'n had bet on her to win. One eye stayed on Riona as the other two moved meaningfully to an unsuspecting Aeron. The race had a quick temper, which usually ended up with body parts being dumped in all corners of the galaxy. Riona gave a meaningful nod to the Pha'n woman and then pointed two fingers briefly to the artery in her neck, indicating she was handling it. The Pha'n made no move to follow, but it was clear the restraint took much unnatural effort on her part.

"There's my soldier," a humanoid man in a feather dress said to Aeron as they passed. "Come back to conscript me?"

The blue-skinned creature next to him laughed heartily in a high-pitched whine. "Con-*strip* you!"

"I see you've been making friends," Riona drawled wryly under her breath, eyeing her sister's uniform. Sometimes she didn't think it was possible they came from the same mother.

"I didn't. They harassed me when I came in to find you and—"

"Yeah, you better keep that affronted-military-voice thing down. Pirates don't take kindly to the law," Riona warned. Aeron was always so literal. Was it possible they even came from the same parents? "You're lucky there was a costume ball tonight and that Federation dress is raging this year with the personal entertainment crowd or you'd have been lynched before you could step through the front door."

"I can assure you, Ri, I didn't want to come here. I didn't have a choice. And I can take care of myself." Aeron gasped. "Personal entertain—did you just say I look like a prostitute?"

"What? No," Riona lied, "you misheard." She saw one of Range's thugs following several paces behind. "Well then, let's not make you wait around here too long. Where's that ship of yours, sis? I can't wait to see it." She tried to hurry Aeron along while smiling for the benefit of Range's men. Joner, a hulking piece of roughened manmeat, had a little bit of a thing for her, but that was one disc this gambler didn't want to have to throw.

"Where are you staying? Don't you need to tell

your ride that you have other arrangements? Or is there luggage we need to pick up?"

Riona thought of her clothes and meager belongings. Everything she had that was worth fighting for she carried on her person at all times. If she managed to give Range and his men the slip, her room is the first place they'd plunder. Besides, thanks to Aeron's untimely interruption, Riona didn't even have the money to pay her room bill—not that the rusted metal hole in the wall could be considered a real room. "I only flew in for the tournament and didn't bring much with me. I'm all yours. Now where's that ship?"

"What is with you?" Aeron demanded, trying to slow down.

"I'm hurt. My sister comes here after how many years and asks *me* for *my* help and now you suspect I'm up to something because I drop everything to help you?" Riona sighed, shaking her head in disapproval. "It's not like you ask me for favors. The least I can do is take you seriously when you do."

"Well, ah, thank you," Aeron said, nodding slowly. "That is very adult of you, Ri. I can see things have apparently changed with you."

"Riona!"

Riona flinched. Range had apparently changed tactics and decided to follow her himself. They had just walked onto the docking platform where all the ships were parked along an open clearing of concrete. Rows of various travel vessels lined up in assigned squares, packed snugly together to maximize the use of the space. A few people milled about, mostly couples in risqué positions and drunken crewmen trying to find a place to pass out now the gambling was winding down. In the main complex behind them, the party raged on and would continue to do so for several more days. That was the beauty of deep space travel. All the travelers were on a different time schedule, and one person's morning was another person's evening, so when they all gathered together time blended into one long planetary party.

"Should we stop? I think someone's trying to get your attention." Aeron tried to point at the main complex.

"No, I think we should go. Is this your ship? The Federation Military vessel? Subtle, sis, very subtle."

"Riona! I know you're not trying to renege on our bet," Range yelled, the sound of his heavy footfalls coming faster.

"Hey, I think that guy——" Aeron insisted.

"We should really get going, as in now," Riona said, grabbing her sister's arm and jerking her the last several feet to the ship.

"You're in trouble, aren't you? I knew it. I knew you hadn't grown up. You're just using me! I was an idiot to think I could—"

"Do you think we could continue this lecture later? That guy isn't trying to ask me out on a date, if you know what I mean." Her words were punctuated by a warning laser blast aimed in their direction. It whizzed past before fizzling into nothingness.

"Are they shooting at us?" Aeron screamed in surprise as she jerked violently to the left to take cover. "Are they insane? What are they thinking? This is a Federation ship. I am a Federation civilian employee!"

Riona actually laughed at her. How could she not? "Where I come from, that's a reason to shoot. No one will care if you're civilian or military bred. Besides, they're only firing warning shots. They're too far behind us to do much damage to the ship. They just want me to know they're not going to forget the debt so easily."

To Aeron's credit, she hurried to press the security code into the ship's panel to open the entry hatch on the bottom. Instantly, a door slid open and a ladder came down from above. Leading the way, she said, "I can't believe you are so careless with money. I should make you go down and face him."

Riona tolerated the lecture as she followed her sister up the ladder. Only when Aeron stopped to take a breath, did she insert, "Unless you have a bag full of space credits you're willing to leave with me, I'm going to have to beg you not to do that. Besides, you give me a lift and I promise I'll help you with whatever you need." Riona wasn't too worried. Her sister's sense of adventure ran toward a really hard logic puzzle, a cup of hot grog and an auto-warm blankie. How much help could the woman really need?

"How much do you owe?" Aeron demanded, hands on hips as she stopped short of going into the cockpit to start the engines.

Riona hit the control button to make the hatch seal shut. "Don't worry about it." She passed her sister to take the pilot's seat and automatically began initiating launch protocols. A viewing screen popped up to show movement on the outside of the ship as a warning before initiating thrusters. Range was there, slamming his fist into the metal side. His anger reverberated loudly from below. The viewing screen sound was off, but she could see his lips moving and didn't need to hear what he was saying to *know* what he was saying.

"Hey, this is my ship. I'll do the flying."

"Ever out fly an angry pirate?" Riona arched a brow. Aeron gave her a dubious look. "That's what

I thought, analyst. Why don't you just strap in and let me handle this boat? The sooner we get out of here, the better our odds of losing him before the chase even starts. And if I know Range, he'll give chase." As if to prove her point, the pirate stopped hitting their ship and turned to run down the docking lot. He disappeared from the viewing screen.

"We come from the same place, you know," Aeron said.

"What are you talking about?" Riona started up the engine, doing a mental check of the buttons and switches as she readied for flight.

"You said where you come from being Federation is a bad thing. That's not true. We come from the same place." Aeron's literal take on life worked well with her militant pursuits...not so well when trying to relate to other humanoids.

"Yeah," Riona drawled absentmindedly, jerking the controls, "a giant minefield of floating rock."

"Our home world was lovely," Aeron defended.

"Until it exploded into a thousand pieces," Riona answered. "I flew near there a few years back. Nothing but blackness. Even most of the meteors seemed to have floated away."

"How can you talk about it like that?"

Riona didn't answer as she brought up the map of Torgan. Three rings spun at odd angles around the brown-gray planet. Grabbing the communicator, she said, "Torgan Ground, this is, ah—" Riona glanced around trying to find a name and then settled for, "—a ship and we're about to take off, so if you don't want us exploding over the docking platform you better clear the air."

"Riona!" Aeron scolded.

"A ship this is Torgan Ground. We need a little more…" The communicator's words faded as Riona turned down the volume and concentrated on getting out of there.

"What?" She feigned innocence as she began the final phases of departure procedures. The ship was a little different than she was used to, but at this point she could fly just about anything as long as it wasn't a giant cruiser or space station. She wasn't too worried. She knew enough about Torgan to know they wouldn't want a ship exploding over their docking lot. They would be liable not only for ruined ships and damage to their facility, but they'd have possible authoritative inquiries into the incident.

Aeron grabbed the communicator and turned the volume back up. "My apologies for the rookie, Torgan Ground. She panicked. This is Federation ship class three cruiser number six-nineteen-twenty requesting you open for an emergency takeoff." Glancing at her sister, she said, "We've got a level nineteen prisoner onboard that we'd like to get out of your sky."

"Federation class three, understood. Clearing sky traffic. You have an open shot into deep space. Scan protocols being activated and ships are being locked down."

"The Federation thanks you for your cooperation, Torgan Ground," Aeron said, shutting the communicator off.

"Level nineteen prisoner?"

"Possible toxic contaminate," Aeron answered.

"Wow, thanks for that," Riona drawled sarcastically, realizing her sister had likened her to infectious waste. Though she had called Aeron a prostitute earlier, so she guessed they were even. "I love you too."

"I just did you a favor. Whoever is chasing you will have to wait for contamination clearance. Standard protocol whenever there is a possible onworld level nineteen contamination."

The ship shook as they began to move. "I'll have to remember that. Thanks for the tip."

"I didn't tell you that so you would—"

Riona purposefully jerked the ship, jarring her sister to the right and then left to get the woman to stop talking. It worked. Aeron stopped lecturing her. "Try to hold on there, sis."

Lights began to blur on the viewing screen and

the ride became smoother. She relaxed some as the surface view faded from the sensors.

"I can't believe you, Ri," Aeron said through gritted teeth. "I'm with you for two seconds and we're already being chased off a planet because you owe money to a space pirate…"

Blarg. Blarg. Blarg. Riona moved her mouth, silently mocking the lecture and not really paying attention to it. She pushed several buttons before turning away from the control panel to let the ship guide itself. "Okay, you got me out here. We're in space. What's so important you had to slum it with the lowlifes?"

"I need your help. I have to get to a planet on the outer edge of the Y quadrant. I can't keep this ship."

Riona arched a brow.

"The planet is called Qurilixen. The Federation has no authority there, and quite frankly little interest in it or the people, but for their mining operations. The Draig and Var people who inhabit the planet keep to themselves and by all reports live quite primitively. About five months ago, I intercepted some data that leads me to believe the people there might be in trouble. The Federation refused to get involved. So long as they get the ore mined on the planet one way or another, they're keeping their hands clean of the whole situation.

But after seeing our home world explode, I can't stand by and watch another race of people get wiped out—especially over something like mining rights. If something happened and I did nothing—"

"So let me get this straight," Riona interrupted. "You left work without permission and you stole a Federation ship, which you now need to ditch because you're heading to a primitive planet in the Y and don't want the military tracking you. And you need my help to get you there."

"Yes." Aeron bit her lip and nodded. "Will you help me?"

A slow smile spread over Riona's lips. "Ah, little sis, I'm so proud right now I might start crying. Of course I'll help you break a bunch of Federation laws." And the fact Range wouldn't dream of looking for her in the Y was a bonus. "Besides, you know me. I'm always up for a little mischief and adventure."

Riona wasn't sure if her sister's resulting expression was grateful or an attempt to hide her disapproval.

To find out more about Michelle's books visit www.MichellePillow.com

ABOUT MICHELLE M. PILLOW

New York Times & *USA TODAY* Bestselling Author

Michelle loves to travel and try new things, whether it's a paranormal investigation of an old Vaudeville Theatre or climbing Mayan temples in Belize. She believes life is an adventure fueled by copious amounts of coffee.

Newly relocated to the American South, Michelle is involved in various film and documentary projects with her talented director husband. She is mom to a fantastic artist. And she's managed by a dog and cat who make sure she's meeting her deadlines.

For the most part she can be found wearing pajama pants and working in her office. There may or may not be dancing. It's all part of the creative process.

Come say hello! Michelle loves talking with readers on social media!

www.MichellePillow.com

facebook.com/AuthorMichellePillow

twitter.com/michellepillow

instagram.com/michellempillow

bookbub.com/authors/michelle-m-pillow

goodreads.com/Michelle_Pillow

amazon.com/author/michellepillow

youtube.com/michellepillow

pinterest.com/michellepillow

COMPLIMENTARY EXCERPTS

THE SAVAGE KING

BY MICHELLE M. PILLOW

Lords of the Var® **Book 1**
A Qurilixen World Novel

Bestselling Cat-shifter Romance Series

Cat-shifting King Kirill knows he must do his duty by his people. When his father unexpectedly dies, it's his destiny to take the throne and all of the responsibility that entails. What he hadn't prepared for is the troublesome prisoner that's now his to deal with.

Undercover Agent Ulyssa is no man's captive. Trapped in a primitive forest awaiting pickup, she's going to make the best out of a bad situation... which doesn't include falling for the seductions of a king.

About *Lords of the Var*® (Books 1-5)

You met their father, King Attor, in Dragon Lords Books 1-4, now meet the Var Princes!

The cat-shifter princes were raised to not believe in love, especially love for one woman, and they will do everything in their power to live up to their father's expectations. Oh, how the mighty will fall.

The Savage King Excerpt

Kirill watched the door to his bedroom open. He'd been sitting in the dark, trying to relieve the stress headache that had built behind his eyes for the last week. The pain started at the base of his skull and radiated up to his temples until he could hardly see straight.

A heavy responsibility had been thrust on his shoulders, a responsibility he really hadn't prepared himself for, the welfare of the Var people. King Attor had not left him in a good position. He'd rallied the people to the brink of war, convinced them that the Draig were their enemy, and even went so far as to attack the Draig royal family.

Kirill wanted to see peace in the land. However, he knew the facts didn't bode well for it. The Draig had a long list of grievances against King Attor and the Var kingdom.

Before his death, the king had ordered an attack on the four Draig princes, all of which ended horribly for the Var. The worst was when Prince Yusef was stabbed in the back, a most cowardly embarrassment for the Var guard who did it. If he hadn't been executed in the Draig prisons, he would've been ostracized from the Var community. Luckily, Prince Yusef survived or they'd already be at battle.

Attor had also arranged for the kidnapping of Yusef's new bride. The Draig Princess Olena had been rescued, or that too would've led to war. The old king had even tried to poison Princess Morrigan, the future Draig queen, on two separate occasions. She too lived. And those were only a few of the offenses Kirill knew about in the few weeks before King Attor's death. He could just imagine what he didn't know.

Kirill sighed, feeling very tired. He'd known since birth that the day would come when he'd be expected to step up and lead the Var as their new king. He just hadn't expected it to be for another hundred or so years. His father had been a hard man, whom he'd foolishly believed was invincible.

"Here kitty, kitty, kitty." His lovely houseguest's whisper drew his complete attention from his heavy thoughts.

Ulyssa bent over like she expected him to answer to the insulting call. He dropped his fingers from his temple into his lap, and a quizzical smile came to his lips. As he watched her, he wasn't sure if he was angered or amused by her words.

"Are you in here, you little furball?" she said, a little louder.

She wore his clothes. Never had the outfit looked sexier. His jaw tightened in masculine interest, as he unabashedly looked her over. All too well did he remember the softness of her body against his and the gentle, offering pleasure of her sweet lips. She'd made soft whimpering noises when he'd touched her, yielding, purring sounds in the back of her throat. Even with the aid of nef, he was surprised by how easily and confidently she melted into him. The Var were wild, passionate people and were drawn to the same qualities in others. He suspected she'd be an untamed lover.

Too bad she'd belonged to his father first. In his mind, that made her completely untouchable though none would dare question his claim if he were to take her to his bed. Technically, by Var law, she belonged to him until he chose to release her. For an insane moment, he thought about keeping her as a lover. He knew he wouldn't, but the thought was entertaining.

Kirill's grin deepened. Ulyssa strode across his home to the bathroom door with an irritated scowl. It was obvious she didn't see him in the darkened corner, watching her. He detected her engaging smell from across the room, the smell of a woman's desire. It stirred his blood, making his limbs heavy with arousal. And, for the first time since his father's death, his headache relieved itself.

"Hum, maybe I'm looking too high. I'm sure there has to be a little cat door here somewhere. Come here, little kitty. Where are you hiding?"

His slight smile fell at her words. It was easy to detect her mocking tone.

"Where's your little kitty door, huh?" Ulyssa whispered to herself, her blue gaze searching around in the dark.

Kirill grimaced in further displeasure. He watched her open the door to his weapons cabinet. Her eyes rounded, and he thought she might take one. She didn't. Instead, she nodded in appreciation before closing the door and continuing her search for an exit.

She stopped at a narrow window by his kitchen doorway. Her neck craned to the side, as she tried to see out over the distance. Kirill knew she looked at the forest. From under her breath, he heard her vehement whisper, "Where exactly did you little fur balls bring me? Ugh, I need to get out of this flea trap, even if I have to fight every one of you cowardly felines to do it. I've fought species twice as big and three times as frightening. A couple of little kitty cats don't scare me."

If this insolent woman wanted to play tough, oh, he'd play. Curling gracefully forward, Kirill shifted before his hands even touched the ground. He let one thick paw land silently on the floor, followed by a second. Short black fur rippled over his tanned flesh, blending him into the shadows. His clothes fell from his body, and he lowered his head as he crept forward. A low sound of warning started in the back of his throat. He was livid.

To find out more about Michelle's books visit www.MichellePillow.com

PLEASE LEAVE A REVIEW

Please take a moment to share your thoughts by scrolling to the end of the document to rate/review this book.
Thank you for reading!

Be sure to check out Michelle's other titles at

www.michellepillow.com